D1464285

Stranger in the House

By ZOA SHERBURNE

Cover design by Ethel Gold

SCHOLASTIC BOOK SERVICES
NEW YORK • TORONTO • LONDON • AUCKLAND • SYDNEY • TOKYO

Copyright © 1963 by Zoa Sherburne. This edition is published by Scholastic Books Services, a division of Scholastic Magazine, Inc., by arrangement with William Morrow & Co., Inc.

18 17 16 15 14 13 12 11 10 9 8 7   5 6 7 8 9/7 0/8

Printed in the U. S. A.

To Herb, with love.

1

AFTERWARD Kathleen remembered every detail of that afternoon which was to mark the crumbling of her old familiar world and the beginning of a strange new one.

She walked home from school with Marge Chessman, who lived across the street from her, and the two girls discussed the play that had been chosen for the end of the school term. Marge, who was interested in dramatics, planned to try out for the leading role.

"Well, of course Evelyn *looks* the part," Marge pointed out generously. "But she can't act worth sour apples."

Kathleen responded with a loyalty that Marge expected. "You look the part as much as she does, and your personality projects better. Even Sister Mary Catherine admits that."

They didn't discuss Kathleen's chances of getting a part. She would probably be a member of the chorus. One year she had been one of the queen's handmaidens and carried the queen's robe. She had had just one line: "Your Majesty, a man approaches on horseback!" But she had been so frightened that she was determined never again to try out for a speaking part. Another year she had been a woodsman. Kathleen and Marge attended an all-girl school, and the girls with short hair usually took the boys' roles.

Marge had long black hair and a dazzling smile, and a voice that reached the back of the balcony. She was always a girl in the school productions, and usually she was the leading lady.

At one time Marge had tried to interest Kathleen in dramatics, but she laughed it off. "Marge, honestly, I'm just not the type."

A bicycle went whizzing by just as they reached the corner, and automatically Kathleen yelled after it. "Wimpy Frazier, you slow down for the crossings or I'll tell Alma!" Her threatening voice did not seem to bother her brother in the least. She watched him swing into the driveway of the big white house and disappear around the garage.

It was like a thousand other unimportant afternoons—the sort of day that left her with nothing to write about when she opened her diary. It wasn't that life was dull, because Kathleen really liked school and her widening circle of friends there. Home was pleasant, too. She loved her father and Wimpy, who was a little pest most of the time, and Alma, who was so much like a parent that sometimes Kathleen had to remind herself that Alma wasn't her mother.

Once a new girl at school had asked Kathleen about the relationship. "She isn't your real mother, is she? Isn't she just the housekeeper?"

Kathleen had to smile at that, because it seemed so silly to think of Alma in that way. "Alma's the one who keeps the roof from caving in," she explained, borrowing one of her father's pet phrases. "My mother's been in a hospital for years and years—Alma takes care of us."

It was as simple as that. Alma takes care of us.

Kathleen said good-bye to Marge at the corner and crossed the street. She walked the rest of the way with quick, impatient steps, because there was something important she wanted to ask Alma before Wimpy came in and claimed her attention.

She went in the front door, and then stopped

and braced herself. The air was full of the smell of fresh gingerbread.

Alma probably didn't realize it herself, but for years and years she had prepared Kathleen for whatever ordeal lay ahead by baking gingerbread. There had been the time the doctor had decided Kathleen's tonsils should come out, the time Kathleen's father was involved in the automobile accident, and the time Wimpy was in the hospital with pneumonia. There was also the time Kathleen failed the examinations that would admit her to music camp, and the afternoon the children learned that their mother was being sent back to the sanatorium. . . .

Kathleen put her books down carefully on the dining-room table and walked out into the kitchen, where Alma was putting dishes into the automatic dishwasher. Usually she was cheerful and smiling when Kathleen came in from school, but this afternoon she hadn't heard the door open and close, so she hadn't had time to put on her normal welcoming smile. It disturbed Kathleen to see her look so grim and preoccupied. For the first time in Kathleen's memory, she looked old.

Not that Alma *was* old. She was the same age as Kathleen's father; as a matter of fact, they had gone to high school together. But this afternoon she looked old.

4

It was a disquieting thought. Usually Kathleen took Alma completely for granted and didn't even think about how she looked or how old she was. She took her father for granted the same way. He was the man who came home for dinner every evening, who doled out allowances to her and Wimpy, and who went over the household accounts with Alma at the end of the month. Occasionally he took them to the movies and to drive-ins, mowed the lawn and trimmed the hedges, and played baseball with Wimpy once in a while. He could be counted on as a chauffeur when she attended school functions, and she liked to introduce him to her friends because he was so good-looking and courteous. She didn't know much about her father's life outside the family. Sometimes he brought his business associates home, and he always seemed proud to tell them that Kathy was his daughter and Wimpy his son. He played golf on Saturday afternoon and sometimes on Sunday after he took them to church. He was very seldom cross and demanding, the way some of her friends' fathers were, and he had a habit of saying, "See what Alma thinks about it," when either Kathleen or Wimpy wanted something.

Alma looked up and saw her standing there in the doorway, and the smile Kathleen had been waiting for was turned on at once. "Well

5

hi," she said. "I didn't hear you come in. There's fresh gingerbread if you want an afterschool snack."

Kathleen nodded. "I know. I smelled it as soon as I opened the door." She wrinkled her nose and then sighed blissfully, because Alma expected her to be pleased. "When I get to heaven, I'm going to have warm gingerbread three times a day."

She could feel Alma's thoughtful gray eyes following her as she cut wedges of the gingerbread and poured two glasses of milk, one for herself and one for Wimpy, who would be exploding into the kitchen at any moment.

He came in just as she put the bottle back in the refrigerator, and dumped his books unceremoniously on the nearest chair. His brown eyes, warm and penetrating like his father's, flew from Kathleen to Alma. "What's the matter?" he demanded abruptly. "What's wrong?"

Alma shrugged. "Nothing is wrong, Greg. Why?"

He scowled a little. "I don't know. When I first walked in I thought there was something the matter—like somebody sick or something." He scratched his head, but his eyes were still suspicious.

It's the gingerbread, Kathleen told him silently. So you're beginning to get the message

6

too. It's the fresh gingerbread—Alma's way of giving us courage and comfort. But courage and comfort for what?

"Oh boy, gingerbread!" Wimpy said, discarding his earlier uneasiness. He came over and scooped up the biggest piece without even washing his hands. Alma didn't object. She went on about her work, and her face was serene and smiling again. Only her eyes betrayed the fact that she was still troubled.

"Do I have to go to the store for anything?" Kathleen asked, just as she always did. "Or should I go up and change my clothes and get started on my homework?"

Alma thought for a second. "I don't believe we need anything, honey. So why not get started on your homework. You, too, young man," she added firmly to Wimpy, who had snatched up a second wedge of gingerbread and was heading for the door. "No television tonight until you've put in at least an hour with the books. Your father wasn't kidding about that."

"Aw, that's just dumb," Wimpy objected. "I don't even have homework every night. Lots of times I get it all done at school."

"Not according to your last report card," she reminded him. "If you don't have any regular assignments, you can read to me while I peel some vegetables. Your reading needs practice.

You don't want to have to go to summer school and break up your whole vacation, do you?" The words were firm enough, but there was something about her voice and something about the way she looked at Wimpy that made Kathleen realize that whatever disturbing wind was blowing would affect Wimpy too.

Her mind slid hastily along the list of possibilities. It couldn't be something wrong with her father, because Alma would have let them know immediately. The time he had been in the automobile accident she had walked to school to tell Kathleen about it before she got the report from someone else and became unduly alarmed. And it couldn't be about her mother, because the last report from the hospital was that she was getting along very well. It couldn't be any special plans canceled, because there were no special plans looming. They hadn't even decided on a vacation yet. If anything was the matter with Chipper or Miss Skylark. . . .

But Miss Skylark, the parakeet, was twitting happily in her cage, and Kathleen had seen their big dog on her way into the house. It couldn't be Chipper, but Kathleen asked to make sure. "How does Chipper look today?" she said. Her brother stared at her as if she had suddenly sprouted a green beard.

"He looks like a dog. What did you expect?"

8

Wimpy took another bite of gingerbread, and said, "Boy! Girls sure do ask the dumbest questions."

Kathleen looked over at Alma, who was getting vegetables from the bottom drawer of the refrigerator. Alma would tell them what was bothering her, but it would have to be in her own good time.

Kathleen went up the stairs and changed from her school uniform to the jeans and shirt she wore around the house. She looked around her room with some satisfaction as she changed. Up until Wimpy was seven, four years ago, they had shared the big nursery at the end of the hall and this had been the guest room, but Alma had pointed out to Kathleen's father that a girl of twelve really ought to have her own room. Wimpy still occupied the nursery, and the room now reflected his exuberant personality. It flaunted banners, pennants, and model planes and cars.

Alma's room was just across the hall. It had originally been the sewing room, but Alma insisted that it was exactly the right size for her needs. Besides, she wanted to be close enough to hear the children in case they cried out during the night. Their father slept in the big downstairs bedroom, and the other downstairs bedroom had always been used as a den. At least it was furnished with a desk, shelves, and books.

Kathleen went down the stairs with her homework and spread her books out at the end of the kitchen table. Presently Wimpy came in with some arithmetic problems and settled down opposite her. He worked with one eye on the clock and a maximum of squirms and mutters, which Alma pretended not to notice. It was early April and baseball practice was just starting, but homework was supposed to come first, and Alma could be surprisingly stubborn about such things.

An hour slipped past, during which a steady stream of small boys knocked at the back door to ask if Wimp could come out and play. At last Wimpy pushed back his chair and bounded to his feet triumphantly. "Hey, I'm all done. *Now* can I go out and play with the other guys?" He addressed the question to Alma who, for the past several minutes, had been sitting on the high stool near the kitchen window, looking out unseeingly at the familiar neighborhood.

"In a moment, Greg." She spoke in such a quiet, faraway voice that Kathleen looked up at once, tensing herself for whatever bad news might be forthcoming.

"I don't see why you always call me Greg," Wimpy declared, as he slapped his books and papers together haphazardly. "Everybody else calls me Wimpy."

Alma smiled. "I know, but Gregory is such a nice name." And then she added, as if she were thinking aloud, "Your mother chose the name."

"Yeah—Gregory Timothy Frazier." Wimpy recited the name with deep disgust.

Alma turned her gentle smile in Kathleen's direction.

"I wanted to tell you something—the two of you—before your father gets home, so that you'll be a little prepared." She paused and took a quick sharp breath, and then folded her hands together in her lap. Kathleen had employed the same trick herself on numerous occasions when she wanted to look calm and unflustered, when she wanted to be sure that her hands didn't betray her by trembling. She waited, anxious to know what Alma had to say but wanting, at the same moment, to run and hide so that she could avoid hearing it.

"Dr. Lundigan called your father this afternoon," Alma went on when she was sure she had their full attention. "I had the call transferred to his office, and I suppose he knew I'd be wondering what it was all about, so he called me back to let me know." She looked at Wimpy, who was still glancing anxiously at the clock on the kitchen wall. "Your mother will be coming home in a couple of weeks. The doctors say that she is well."

Wimpy looked startled. "You mean she's going to live *here*?"

"Of course. She's your mother. This is her home."

"I thought she was going to stay in that place forever and ever," Wimpy said bluntly. "She won't like it here. She doesn't even know us any more. The last time we went to see her—" He stopped abruptly and shut his lips. "She scares me, Alma. I don't want her to come back."

"When you saw your mother three years ago, she was very ill, Greg. Now that she's well, she's eager to be home and have her family together again."

Wimpy looked vaguely mollified. "Well, I guess it'll be O.K. Is it all right if I go out and play now?"

"Yes. Of course. Put your books in your room first, and there are some bananas in the bowl on the sideboard so you can keep up your strength until dinnertime."

Wimpy's appetite was a standing family joke. Keeping up Wimpy's strength from meal to meal, his father often declared, would some day land them all on a poor farm.

When Wimpy had clattered off the porch Alma turned to Kathleen, who was still staring down at her World Problems notebook. "You haven't said anything, Kit." Kit was Alma's special name for her, and the way she used it amounted to an endearment. "Does that mean that you aren't really surprised?"

Kathleen still didn't look up. "*Surprised* is scarcely the word. *Stunned* would be more like it." She closed her books together firmly, knowing that this was something she and Alma had to discuss alone. "How did Father seem to take the news?"

"Well . . . he was pleased, naturally," Alma said slowly. "Surprised, of course, and excited. . . ."

"I don't believe it," Kathleen broke in unsteadily. "I don't believe that he was pleased or excited. I think . . . I think that he's probably just *sick* inside—the way I am."

Alma came around the table swiftly, and her arm was firm and comforting around Kathleen's shoulder as she pulled her head against her and patted her hair. "Honey, you don't really mean that. You're glad she's better. She's your mother."

"I don't even know her," Kathleen said desperately. "I can't even remember what she looked like, except in little flashes once in a while, or when I look at the pictures Dad keeps around the house. I must have been eight the last time she went away. Wimpy was only three. It's been eight whole years. How can she expect to come back and start being our mother when we're used to your being our mother all this time?"

Alma's arm tightened. "Kit, dear, I am the housekeeper, remember?"

"You aren't the housekeeper," Kathleen told her steadily. "You know perfectly well that you're a lot more than that. You're the one who nursed me through the measles and chicken pox and sent me to dancing school and made my costumes. You're the one who made my graduation dress and attended the P.T.A. workshop and ran the hot-dog sale for the Girl Scouts. You help us with our homework and give me advice about how to talk to boys, and you were the one who helped Wimpy make his racer...."

Alma walked away then. She went back to the stove, turned the heat lower under the vegetables, and looked at the clock. Then she started to get the dishes from the cupboard. "She's coming home, Kathleen. She's been very ill and quite lonely. And she has missed her family."

"You're just guessing about that," Kathleen said. "When Father took us there, to the hospital, she didn't even remember us. She cried and told us to go away, and she wouldn't even look at Father."

14

"I know, honey, but that was a long time ago. They've found new ways to help people like your mother. She'll be a completely different person."

"I don't want a completely different person," Kathleen said. "I just want you and Father and Wimpy and me, being together. Being a family."

Alma looked at her sternly. "But we aren't a real family. I work here. I love all of you and I want what's best for you—for all of you. Helen is your mother. You seem to be forgetting that."

Kathleen was silent for a moment before asking the question that was uppermost in her mind.

"What about you, Alma? What will you do when Mother's home again?"

"Your father has asked me to stay on for a while," Alma said, without turning from the cupboard. "And I've told him I'll stay for as long as any of you needs me. But Helen may have her own ideas about that. You know the old saying about no house being large enough for two women."

"What if she . . . what if Mother doesn't want you to stay?" Kathleen forced herself to ask the question, although it was bound to be painful to both of them. "The last time she was home—" She broke off and Alma turned her head to look at her steadily.

"She wasn't responsible, Kathleen. She really didn't know what she was saying. She probably doesn't even remember it. Somehow she convinced herself that I was her enemy. It's all long ago and forgotten."

"I don't think it's forgotten at all," Kathleen said. "I don't think you've forgotten a single word she said, or Father either. I was only eight years old, and *I* remember."

Kathleen got up, taking her books with her, and left the kitchen. Slowly she went up the stairs and into her bedroom. She was startled when she saw her face in the mirror over her dressing table; she looked so white and wild-eyed.

She could hear Wimpy and some of his friends shouting and laughing on the vacant lot across the street next to the Chessmans' house. She went to the window and looked out, pressing her forehead against the cool glass. It must be wonderful to be eleven years old, to be able to go on as if nothing had changed, when your entire world was being turned upside down and wrong side out. But Wimpy had said, "She scares me. I don't want her to come back." Remembering this Kathleen felt a quick thrust of pity.

It was impossible to think ahead, to try and foresee what this new development might mean to all of them. Embarrassment, of course.

It was only occasionally that Kathleen was called upon to explain that her mother was in a hospital—a mental hospital. Over the years it had become such an accepted thing that people had long since stopped talking about it. Kathleen's mother was very ill; she would probably never return to a normal life. People had even stopped talking about how "unsuitable" it was for an unmarried woman like Alma Prescott to take over the raising of another woman's family.

Kathleen picked up the picture of her mother from the top of her desk and studied it closely. She couldn't seem to feel anything, nothing at all, except a vague unrest and unhappiness. She couldn't remember when her mother was like other mothers. It was shortly after Wimpy was born that she had started having the spells of depression that had become progressively worse. Of course, as Kathleen's father had explained over and over, it had really started a long time before that. Her mother had never been very strong, and she was high-strung and emotional. The shock of losing both her mother and father in an automobile accident had added to her tension and nervousness.

But Kathleen had overheard different versions, less tolerant versions, as time went on. Mrs. Jenson, who had been one of the first of a long line of housekeepers and mother's helpers, was inclined to tell everyone, from the laundryman to the grocery clerks to the man who delivered the mail, about the trouble at the Fraziers' house.

"That man is a saint, that's what he is," Kathleen heard Mrs. Jenson call her father on more than one occasion. "How he puts up with that woman is more than I can understand. You'd think a grown woman with two lovely children and a husband who waits on her hand and foot would count her blessings. But what does she do? Moans and cries and takes to her bed with a headache whenever the work piles up or the children get sick or anything that doesn't exactly suit Her Highness comes up."

Mrs. Jenson paid scant attention to the doctor's definition of Helen Frazier's illness. "Insecure, is she?" she sniffed. "Lazy is more like it. And as for these weeping spells—just to get more attention. Her folks spoiled her rotten. Even after she was married, her mother was over here doing her work and taking care of the baby and telling Helen that she was delicate and ought to take it easy."

Yes, Kathleen had learned a lot about her mother from the Mrs. Jensons around town, but as the years went on and Alma took charge

18

they had managed to put all the unpleasantness and speculation in the background.

It was only a year after her first trip to the hospital that Kathleen's mother was allowed to return home for a probationary period. The children had learned by this time to get along very nicely without their mother and Kathleen had recognized, even at the age of eight, that having her mother come back had been a tragic mistake.

For the first week end it had been very gay, like having a charming guest with them for a visit, but when the novelty of being home again had worn thin their mother had retreated into her own private world where the children were intruders. She hated it when Wimpy cried, she was afraid of Chipper, who was just a puppy then, and she snapped at Kathleen when the little girl teased to go out and play with the neighbor children. But the worst part of it was that she hated Alma. Soon after she came home, Alma went away to live with some friends of hers in another city, and from that day on things started to fall apart. Both the children cried when Alma left, and this at first angered and then frightened their mother.

One morning she just didn't get out of bed. Kathleen's father had already left for work and Kathleen was supposed to go to school, but she knew that she couldn't leave Wimpy alone with her mother, who was whispering to herself and paying absolutely no attention to Kathleen's questions or the little boy's tears. A neighbor woman finally came and took the two youngsters to her house, and after that Alma was home again and peace was blessedly restored.

The doctor came and went and Kathleen heard him talking to her father in terms that she was too young to understand. "We'll try it for another week," Kathleen's father said finally, and the doctor went away shaking his head.

It was soon after that that her mother went away again, but not before the terrible scene when she had screamed and raged at Alma, accusing her of all sorts of horrible things only partly understood by the little girl who was a silent but horrified witness. Wimpy hadn't understood either, but he knew that he was frightened. He stood in his crib screaming at the top of his lungs while all the shouting and crying was going on.

Finally Kathleen's mother had locked herself in the bathroom and refused to come out. Her father, summoned from his work by a frantic Alma, had climbed to the second story and forced his way into the bathroom window.

It was her most vivid memory of her mother.

Kathleen heard her father's car turn into the driveway. She put the photograph of the stranger who was her mother back on the desk, brushed at her hair, and tried to turn up the corners of her mouth into a smile.

And then, just as she was starting down the stairs, she remembered that she had hurried home from school to talk to Alma about something important. It had really seemed terribly important this afternoon, but now, no matter how hard she thought about it, she couldn't remember what it was.

2

HER FATHER looked up and saw her at the head of the stairs. "Hi, Duchess," he said, just as usual, and then he picked up the mail from the desk and leafed through it as he did every evening.

Kathleen said, "Hello, Dad," and came down the stairs.

From the kitchen came busy sounds and the murmur of Alma's voice advising Wimpy to get washed up for dinner. Wimpy always headed for the house the moment he saw his father's car round the corner. He came into the hallway now, grinning his urchin grin.

"We clobbered 'em," he told his father happily, "twelve to three."

"Good for you!" his father said.

Wimpy clattered up the stairs to get washed for dinner. Presently Kathleen's father went into his room, and Kathleen went out into the kitchen to help set the table and do the last-minute things.

There was beef stew for dinner. Kathleen and Wimpy weren't especially fond of beef stew, but it was their father's favorite dinner, and Kathleen found herself wondering if perhaps this wasn't the equivalent of the fresh gingerbread Alma baked for her and Wimpy.

They sat down at the table, and Wimpy mumbled the blessing before they started to eat.

"Smells elegant," Kathleen's father said, and smiled at Alma as she placed the heaping plate before him.

They ate for a few moments in unaccustomed silence. Normally Kathleen was full of small talk about school and Alma reported the funny things that had happened around the neighborhood. Wimpy, of course, talked of nothing but baseball these days.

When the silence had become brooding, Kathleen's father looked up and caught her eye. "I suppose Alma told you the good news," he said. "About your mother coming home."

It was hard to read from his expression or his tone what he was really feeling. Kathleen framed her answer carefully. "Yes. She told us. Mother . . . Mother must be terribly excited."

"I expect so. I thought we could call the hospital later on this evening. If we talk to her about coming home, it will seem a little more real to all of us."

"Will they let her take calls?" Kathleen asked, and could have chopped her tongue off the moment the thoughtless words were said. There had been a long time when her mother wasn't allowed to have calls from the family, and more than once, when permission had been granted, she had refused to talk to them.

"Yes, she can have calls," Kathleen's father said. "In fact it was Dr. Lundigan who suggested it." He seemed willing to let the matter rest after that, and they went on with dinner, although Kathleen's beef stew seemed suddenly without flavor.

When the dishes were out of the way, Kathleen asked if she might go down to the library for a while. Wimpy immediately wanted to go, too.

"You don't have to tag along everywhere I go," Kathleen told him. "You're like the shadow in the poem who 'goes in and out with me. . . .'"

"I have to get some books to do book reports on," Wimpy protested. "How's a kid supposed to do his schoolwork if his family makes him stay home all the time?"

"You don't even read the books," Kathleen said. "You just make a book report from what it says on the jacket, and that's cheating."

"It is not," Wimpy said hotly. "All the kids do it that way. Anyway, *almost* all the kids."

"What about those two books you got for Christmas?" Alma broke in smoothly. "The ones about the boys in Alaska. You read those books and liked them. I remember your telling me about them."

"But I read those books for fun," Wimpy told her. "They don't count."

"Of course they count. Your teacher will be glad to know that you're reporting on something you really enjoyed reading."

Wimpy still looked doubtful. "Are you sure, Alma?"

Alma paused a moment. "Well, if I were a teacher, I'd like to have that kind of book report turned in. Run and get the books, and I'll jot down the titles and authors so Kathleen can ask the librarian about them."

Alma almost always had a ready solution to these arguments between brother and sister. Wimpy went off to get his books and didn't even notice that he had been talked out of his trip to the library.

Kathleen called Marge and they walked to the library together, stopping on the way to pick up some things at the drugstore for Marge's mother, who was always trying out some new kind of medicine. "It's her sinus this time," Marge explained airily. "Last week it was her back, and the week before that it was her lungs. Mother finds something new every day."

Kathleen looked at her friend unsmilingly. "I don't think that's very funny," she said.

Marge giggled. "Well, I do, and so does Aunt Celia. She's always teasing Mother about being a hypochondriac."

"I don't think it's very nice of your Aunt Celia either," Kathleen said shortly. "And anyway, *you* should talk—you're always coming down with a cold when it's time for tests, or getting a splitting headache all of a sudden."

Marge shrugged. "I know. I expect it runs in the family. All the Chessman women enjoy poor health." She gave Kathleen a sharp glance. "I don't see why you should be such a crab tonight. If you didn't want me to come to the library with you, why did you invite me?"

Kathleen relented. She put her hand through Marge's arm and squeezed it remorsefully. "I'm sorry. I guess I am behaving like a crab, but I have things on my mind."

Marge's smile forgave her readily. "Did you ask Alma whether you could go on that overnight to the state capital?" she asked.

Kathleen shook her head. "No. I was going to, but I forgot. Anyway, I couldn't—not now."

"Why not?" Marge demanded. "It's a class project and it'll cost next to nothing. Just the room at the Y and bus fare. I think it'll be a ball."

"I'm sure it will," Kathleen said. "But I won't be able to go this time. My mother is coming home in a couple of weeks. We just heard about it today."

Marge glanced at her warily. "You mean for a visit or for always?"

"She's coming home to stay," Kathleen said firmly. "She's been getting better for a long, long time. Even her letters sound more like . . . as if she's really interested in things." She made a vague, all-encompassing gesture, and Marge nodded to show that she understood. "So now the doctors have pronounced her perfectly well, and she's coming home."

"Are you happy about it?" Marge asked. Then she added, "I mean, you don't sound very happy."

"I'm still more surprised than anything," Kathleen said. "The news came suddenly." And then she smiled. "But naturally I'm happy that she's well again."

She was glad she had told Marge about her mother coming back, because the first thing Mrs. Webster, the librarian, said was, "Well, Kathleen, I hear that your dear mother is coming home. Isn't that lovely?"

Kathleen was too astonished to think of a suitable answer, but fortunately Mrs. Webster never waited for anyone to answer anything. She just went rippling along like Tennyson's brook. When someone else claimed her attention, she drifted off, leaving Kathleen and Marge to select the books they wanted.

"That's the trouble with this town," Marge whispered. "Everyone knows everybody else's business. You'd think we were all hooked up on the same party line."

But except for being curious about where Mrs. Webster had obtained her information, Kathleen didn't really care. It would be a relief if she didn't have to make the announcement over and over in the coming weeks. "My mother has been released from the sanatorium. My mother will be coming home soon."

They stopped at the malt shop on the way home and Marge, who said she felt blissfully rich, treated to chocolate sodas. She did a lot of baby-sitting. which gave her extra money, and besides that she had just had a birthday.

"I really ought to be getting home," Kathleen said, when they had been sitting in the booth talking and laughing and listening to the music of the jukebox for almost an hour. "I told Alma I was just going to pick up some books and come right back."

"Oh, Alma knows you won't get into any

trouble," said Marge calmly. "And your father is probably watching some cowboy show and hasn't even missed you."

Kathleen resisted the impulse to say that her father didn't watch TV, except for newscasts and things like that. All the girls at school complained about how their fathers watched cowboy shows, and she was almost embarrassed about having a father who didn't fit into the prescribed pattern.

"Your father is a real brain, isn't he?" one of the girls at school had said once, when an article under the by-line *Robert D. Frazier* had appeared in an industrial magazine.

Kathleen had brushed the compliment aside, just as if she weren't proud of her father, but the girl had pursued the subject. "I guess he must make a lot of money," she observed tactlessly. "But then he'd have to, what with keeping your mother in that hospital, and paying a full-time housekeeper and everything."

It was the kind of remark that Kathleen heard often. She knew that they were different from other families, but the difference didn't bother her.

Marge was nudging her with her elbow. "Don't look now," she whispered excitedly, "but Bruce Hadley just walked in with another boy, and they're looking this way."

"I really do have to be getting home,"

Kathleen said firmly. She scrambled to her feet just as Bruce reached the booth.

"Well, hello," he said, and his voice made Kathleen's knees turn to butter. "Were you going somewhere?"

"I have to go home," Kathleen said, and even to her own ears she sounded hopelessly infantile. "We were just supposed to go to the library and then straight home."

His eyes brightened. She had the feeling that Bruce was enjoying her discomfort. "But you can't go straight home," he pointed out. "You have to turn a couple of corners, don't you?"

She gave him the smile he expected, and then turned to Marge again. "I'm sorry, Margie, but I really do have to go. Thanks for the soda and everything."

"How about you?" Bruce turned his attention from Kathleen to Marge. "Are you going to brush us off, too, or can we sit down and talk to you for a while?" And then, remembering his manners, he indicated the other boy with a curt nod of his head. "Oh hey, this is Swede Henson. He's new in town. A football hero, no less. Swede, this is Kathleen Frazier just leaving. And the one who's staying is Margie Chessman."

Kathleen glanced back over her shoulder as she left the malt shop. Bruce had slipped into the seat beside Marge, and the boy he had introduced as Swede was sitting across the table from them. None of them seemed to know or care that she was leaving.

She started home slowly. Then she suddenly remembered—her father had said they would call the hospital and talk to her mother this evening. She hurried her steps until she was almost running, but she knew that she was too late. They had to call the hospital before nine-thirty, and at nine-thirty she had still been sitting in the booth at the malt shop drinking a soda and giggling with Marge and putting off going home. She had the oddest feeling that maybe she hadn't forgotten at all, that she had just pushed the thought about telephoning her mother into the back of her mind so that she wouldn't have to be there when they made the call.

She burst into the house a few moments later and saw that the hands of the clock stood at quarter of ten. Her father, who had been reading *Time* magazine, looked up with a question in his dark eyes.

"Oh, Dad, I'm sorry," she said a trifle breathlessly. "Marge treated me to a soda after we were through at the library, and time just seemed to evaporate. I forgot about the call to the hospital until I was on my way home again."

He closed the magazine. "It doesn't matter,

31

Kathleen. We can call tomorrow just as well."

"You didn't call?" She couldn't have explained the way her heart seemed to miss a beat. Relief? Disappointment? It was hard to tell which feeling washed over her.

"No, I didn't call. I thought we'd wait until we were all together."

Kathleen kissed her father good night, he went back to his magazine, and she went out into the kitchen to see what Alma was doing. She found her setting up the lunch sacks for the next day and opening a can of fruit for breakfast. Alma never left anything for the last minute if she could help it.

"Did you get the books you wanted?" she asked. When Kathleen nodded, Alma added, "That's fine. You can start reading them tomorrow when you aren't so tired." It was a tactful way of reminding Kathleen that it was getting on toward her bedtime.

But up in her room, Kathleen didn't get ready for bed immediately. She couldn't help wishing that she hadn't dashed away from the malt shop when Bruce Hadley came in with his friend. The others were probably still there, laughing and talking and having a good time. Margie never seemed to have any trouble knowing what to say to boys, the way Kathleen did. It was one of the reasons that she was so glad Marge had chosen her for a friend. Maybe after a while some of her poise and spontaneous gaiety might rub off on Kathleen.

But they had been best friends for almost four years and it hadn't happened yet. Maybe it never would. It was a little depressing to be practically seventeen and a junior in high school and still not have any of the social graces.

She turned off the lights and went over to look out the window toward Marge's house. The front porch light was still on. That meant that Margie wasn't in yet. It was past ten-thirty, and she was supposed to be in the house before that on school nights, but neither of the Chessmans was strict about enforcing this curfew. Margie pretty much came and went as she pleased.

"Maybe if Dad and Alma weren't so strict about my being home at a certain—" she started to think, and then dismissed the excuse as completely unfair. It certainly wasn't their fault that she became tongue-tied whenever Bruce Hadley looked at her.

Bruce went to the regular high school and she saw him only occasionally, but at one time, when both of them were in the sixth grade, Bruce had been her secret love. No one knew about it, she hadn't even told Margie, but that year she had given Bruce a valentine. She didn't walk right up and hand it to him, of course. There had been a big heart-shaped box in the classroom, and her valentine had gone into it, along with all the others. She didn't sign the card, but she printed *Bruce* in bold, black letters on the envelope, and when all the valentines were distributed that day, she watched from under lowered lashes while he tore open the envelope and read the card.

It was a beautiful lacy valentine that had cost twenty-five cents, but Bruce had laughed as uproariously as if it had been a comic card, and then he had looked directly across the room at Kathleen, who pretended to be very busy reading her own valentines. She had the horrible sinking conviction that he *knew* she had sent him the flowery declaration of her love. She had managed to erase from her memory the tender message that had been printed on the card, but she knew that she would never be able to forget how Bruce had laughed when he read it.

She was still standing by the window looking out when Marge and the two boys came along the street toward the Chessmans' house. They stood and talked for a moment by the gate, and then Marge flew up the walk and into the house. Bruce paused to light a cigarette, and Kathleen could see his profile quite clearly in the brief flare of the match. Then he turned his head and looked across at the Fraziers' house, lifting his eyes unerringly to the window where Kathleen stood watching.

She stepped back hurriedly before she remembered that he couldn't possibly see her, since the room was in total darkness. But perhaps he sensed that she was standing there.

The next time she saw Bruce she wouldn't run away, she promised herself solemnly as she got ready for bed. It was stupid and childish to let that long-ago valentine stand between them—and how could she even be sure that Bruce knew she had sent it? If he came into the malt shop again when she was there, she wouldn't even wait for him to come over to the booth. She'd wave and say, "Hi, Bruce," as if they were old friends. And when he came over to talk to her, she'd think of something gay and memorable to say, so that he'd think about it afterward and wonder why he'd never noticed what an attractive girl she was.

It was a comforting thought. But then she remembered again that her mother was coming home, and the small shadow that had hovered over her all evening seemed to grow and mushroom into something strange and sinister.

3

Her father decided, sometime during the following week, that instead of driving up to Blakely, where the hospital was located, he would take the train. "A long drive might be too tiring for your mother just now," he explained to Kathleen, as seriously as if she had been another grownup. "On the train we'll all be more relaxed."

"We?" Kathleen asked in a very small voice, and he nodded matter-of-factly.

"Yes, I thought you might go up with me. Unless—He looked at her searchingly. "Unless you'd rather not. . . ."

"Oh no. I'd love to go with you," she protested quickly—too quickly. "When will we be going?"

"The week end after this one," her father said. "We can go up on Friday evening. Dr. Lundigan's wife would like to have us spend the night at their house, and then in the morning we can go up to the hospital and check your mother out with plenty of time to catch the afternoon train for home."

He was watching her so closely that Kathleen knew some further expression of her readiness to accompany him was expected. "Mother sounded just like her old self on the telephone," she said. "You're right. This way will be better. She won't be getting acquainted with us all at once. You and I will have her to ourselves for a while before she sees Wimpy and Alma and all her old friends."

Her father nodded and fumbled in his pocket for his pipe. He never smoked a pipe unless he was trying to calm himself. It was, Kathleen thought, a dead giveaway that he was more troubled about all this than he cared to let her know.

When he finally had the pipe going, he sat down, not in his usual chair, but on the davenport beside Kathleen. After a moment, he reached over and patted her hand awkwardly, not quite looking at her. "It will be difficult for a while," he said, "for all of us."

37

"I know," she said, and then added, "but we'll manage. We'll manage beautifully."

He gave her a quick smile. "Of course we will."

The week passed quickly, one day melting into the next like ocean waves overlapping one another. But the tension was there, growing and building until you could feel it—until you could almost reach out and touch it.

Alma, who was always the easiest person in the world to get along with, was suddenly demanding and impossible to please. Kathleen didn't mind when Alma turned a large share of the cooking and cleaning over to her, but it was bewildering that all her efforts rated no praise, that nothing was quite good enough to satisfy.

Gradually it dawned on her that Alma was schooling her for the time when she would be expected to be a real help to her mother—when she might conceivably find herself running the house almost singlehanded. It was a frightening thought, because it meant that Alma was looking ahead toward the time when she would no longer be with them.

One afternoon, when Alma was cleaning the refrigerator and Kathleen was baking cookies, they talked about it.

"Alma, if you did decide to leave us, after Mother is home again, where would you go?"

"I'd go back to Maryland," Alma said, so promptly that Kathleen knew she had given the matter a great deal of serious thought.

"Why Maryland?" Kathleen wanted to know. "I thought all your family had moved away from there ages ago."

"Not quite all," Alma replied. "I still have a brother there, and some cousins. Besides, it might be fun to go back after all these years and revisit the scenes of my long-lost youth. I was only twelve or thirteen when we left."

Kathleen arranged a last row of cookies on a pan and slipped it into the oven. "But you promised that you'd stay as long as any of us needed you," she said.

Alma looked across at her and her gray eyes glistened with a brightness that threatened tears. "Yes, I promised," she said. "As long as any of you need me."

Kathleen looked at her searchingly. "We'll always need you. I can't imagine getting along without you any more than I can imagine getting along without Dad or Wimpy."

Alma gave her a smile and then turned away quickly. "Thanks, honey," she said. "That was very nicely put."

Kathleen shook her head. "I'm not trying to pass out compliments. I guess . . . I guess I'm a little scared."

39

"Of course you are," Alma said. "So am I. And so is your mother, most likely."

Kathleen stared at her. "You mean that maybe she might not *want* to come home?" She couldn't help the feeling of hope that just saying the words gave her. Because if her mother didn't want to come home and wasn't happy with them, maybe she wouldn't stay.

But if Alma suspected what Kathleen was thinking, she gave no sign. "She probably doesn't have a choice," Alma said calmly. "A hospital is for sick people, and she is well. The doctors believe this, and so she is being sent home. It's as simple as that."

"What if . . . what if it doesn't work out?" Kathleen forced herself to ask at last.

Alma's shrug was expressive. "Your father mentioned something about a three-month visit, before she is formally discharged. It's unusual, but Dr. Lundigan feels that this is not an ordinary case."

At school the news had filtered out. Kathleen's mother, who had been hospitalized for years and years, was coming home at last. The nuns who taught at St. Leo's were especially happy about it. They simply took it for granted that, of course, Kathleen wanted her mother home again, and that Mrs. Frazier's recovery was a direct answer to prayer.

"Is she liable to get funny spells again?" Beth Graham wanted to know.

"Kathleen's mother never had anything like that," Marge interrupted firmly. "She just got very depressed, and the doctors thought she'd be better off in a hospital, that's all."

"I've heard that they give people like that tranquilizers and stuff," another girl chimed in helpfully. "The papers are always printing articles about how the doctors have done such wonderful things for mental illness."

Kathleen was grateful for the way they tried to make things easier for her, even though she was aware that they did a lot of whispering when she wasn't around. The nuns went to great pains to explain that mental illness was just like any other disorder—once a cure was found, the patient recovered. "After all, we wouldn't dream of criticizing a friend who was afflicted with polio. We'd be willing and anxious to do anything we could for him."

Yes, the nuns helped to smooth the way for Kathy. At his school, Wimpy didn't fare quite as well. But Wimpy was tough, and he could fight back. One afternoon he came home with quite a few scratches and an eye that was beginning to darken. He'd been in a fight with a boy who had referred to Wimpy's mother as a "kook."

"My mother says that your mother is a real

kook," the boy had said, and made winding motions beside his ear to illustrate. "How come they let her out of the loony bin? Is she safe to run around loose?"

"You should have just ignored him," Alma said indignantly, as she daubed antiseptic on the scratches. "I don't understand what makes children so cruel to each other."

"I hope you beat him to a pulp," Kathleen said. "He's nothing but a smart aleck and a troublemaker."

"Of course I didn't beat him up. He's *that much* bigger than I am," Wimpy protested. "He made me say uncle right away. But now he won't tease me about my mother being a kook again."

"Why not?" Kathleen asked. "Why won't he?"

"Because he already beat me up," Wimpy explained patiently. "He wouldn't beat me up twice about the same thing."

He went off to play with Chipper then, and seemed to forget the entire incident. When his father asked him at the dinner table how he had collected the black eye and all the scratches, Wimpy explained that he had been wrestling with another kid.

An hour or so after dinner Marge called and invited Kathleen to come over for the evening. Usually Marge just yelled across the street. There was something a little mysterious about her subdued voice and the fact that she had called on the telephone. "Just tell Alma that you and I are getting together to do some homework," she suggested lightly. "Tell her you won't be very late."

"But I already did my homework," Kathleen pointed out. "Why don't you come over here?"

Marge laughed, a put-on, husky laugh that she had learned from a movie star. "No, you come over here," she said. "You can say we're listening to some new records." She hung up before Kathleen could ask any more questions. Puzzled, Kathleen went out on the front porch to ask Alma if she might run over to Marge's place for a while.

Alma looked up at her gravely. "I suppose it will be all right. Did you mention it to your father?"

Kathleen shrugged. "Oh, Father's in the den surrounded by mountains of important-looking papers. And anyway, he'd just say to ask you." She waited, but still Alma hesitated.

"Aren't you going to change into a clean blouse and skirt?" Alma asked carefully.

Kathleen looked amazed. "For heaven's sake, why? It's just Marge. It's just across the street."

Alma glanced over at the Chessmans' house and then at Kathleen again. "I just thought it might be a party or something. A couple of boys parked their car down on the next block and

43

walked back and went into Marge's a little while ago."

Kathleen nodded thoughtfully. "So that's what she was being so mysterious about. Maybe I will change into my skirt and sweater—these jeans look pretty awful." She paused and looked at Alma seriously. "Or I could call Marge back and tell her I'm not coming."

"Do you want to do that?"

"I guess not. Not really." She couldn't tell Alma that she was afraid one of the boys would turn out to be Bruce Hadley. And anyway, she couldn't go on avoiding Bruce for the rest of her life, could she? She lifted her chin. "Maybe I will go over for a little while—if it's all right with you." She darted back into the house and up the stairs to put on her new pink skirt and dyed-to-match sweater.

Walking across the street to Marge's house, she was aware that her heart was hammering, but she hoped that she looked cool and unruffled as she rang the bell. Mr. Chessman opened the door for her, and she smiled at him.

"Oh," he said. "It's you, Kathleen. I thought it was the paper boy." He put his wallet back into his pocket and let her in. "Marge and the other kids are down in the recreation room. Tell them to keep the record player turned down, will you? Mrs. Chessman is having another of her migraine headaches." He went back to the television set, and Kathleen went down the stairs to join the others.

"Hi, come on down," Marge called gaily. She was wearing one of her most becoming dresses and she had done something different to her hair, twisting it up on top. But her eyes widened in surprise when she saw that Kathleen was wearing her new sweater set. "You know Swede and Bruce, of course."

Kathleen looked at the two boys sitting cross-legged on the floor beside the record player. "Yes, I know Swede and Bruce," she said.

Bruce looked up and waved his Coke bottle at her. "Come on down and join the party," he said, and motioned to the footstool beside him. "Marge has some real square discs here. How about this one—*The Pennsylvania Polka?* And here's another, same vintage—*Dancing in the Dark.*"

"I told you. They're my mother's records," Marge explained.

Swede got to his feet awkwardly and mumbled something that passed for hello. It occurred to Kathleen that he was probably very shy.

"Here's a Glenn Miller number," Marge announced brightly, and put the record on the machine while Swede slumped back on the floor in an attitude of complete boredom.

Bruce got up, pulling Marge with him, and they started to dance.

Kathleen sat on the footstool, her hands twisted in her lap. To look at Swede would mean that she expected him to ask her to dance, but she didn't want to look at the dancing couple either, so she leaned forward, watching the spinning disc, and tried to assume a rapturous expression. She wished bitterly that she had followed her first instinct and stayed at home. She just wasn't very good with boys; she could never think of gay and sprightly things to say, the way other girls could.

Ages later the record stopped, and Bruce came over to flip it to the other side. "Your turn," he said imperiously, and held out his hand to help her to her feet.

"I'm not a very good dancer," Kathleen heard herself babbling, but Bruce ignored her protests and swung her into the dance easily. At first she was so flustered that her feet wouldn't cooperate, but after a moment her natural sense of rhythm came to her rescue, and she didn't have to think about the steps.

"There. That wasn't so bad, was it?" He stopped and looked down at her thoughtfully when the music ended.

"Not . . . not bad at all," she confessed a trifle breathlessly.

Bruce looked at Swede, who was doggedly

ignoring Marge's attempts to lure him onto the dance floor. "Come on, Swede," he said. "Dance this one with Kathy."

Somewhat to Kathleen's surprise Swede got to his feet, and when the music started they danced—if you could call it dancing. Swede shuffled along awkwardly. Suddenly his knees bumped against her and he laughed, a short bark of embarrassed laughter. Kathleen gritted her teeth and struggled to keep step. They danced for half an hour, with Kathy biting back her disappointment and assuring Swede that he was really doing just fine—while Bruce danced time after time with Margie.

"Hey, we go great together," Swede announced happily after the first twenty or thirty times around. "Let's try it again."

And Kathleen, concentrating on keeping her feet out from under Swede's enormous shoes, had time only to nod and grimace in agreement.

She could have cried with relief when she heard the cuckoo clock in the upstairs hallway sound ten. "I have to go home now," she said at once. "I promised Alma I'd be home by ten."

"Who did you promise?" Swede demanded. "Can't you call and say you'll be a few minutes late?"

"No, I can't," Kathleen said, and smiled to soften the words. She turned to Marge, who was still dancing with Bruce, and raised her voice so she could be heard over the music. "I have to run along now, Margie. See you tomorrow."

Marge nodded dreamily. "See you tomorrow," she echoed. "Swede will walk home with you."

"That won't be at all necessary," Kathleen protested, but Swede clutched her arm and steered her toward the stairs.

"Sure I'll walk home with you."

Bruce looked after them, grinning his lazy grin. "Good night," he called. "Be good, you two."

Swede walked across the street with her. She had managed to pull her arm free and she walked rapidly, but he was right there at her elbow when she opened the door.

"Good night," she said. "Thanks for walking home with me."

He grinned and bobbed his head. Kathleen decided belatedly that maybe he was all right, just a little clumsy. "Thank *you*," he said, "for the dancing lessons and everything. When Marge said she had a friend who'd be glad to tow me around, I didn't think it'd be anyone like you."

Kathleen bit back an indignant retort. After all, it wasn't his fault that he was such a poor dancer. He was still standing there when she closed the door firmly behind her.

Alma looked up from a television show

when Kathleen paused briefly in the doorway. "Have fun?" she asked.

Kathleen shrugged. "It was O.K." She went into the den where her father was humped over some paper work and kissed him good night.

"You look pretty," he told her. "Did you have a nice time?"

"Very nice," she assured him gravely.

It was a funny thing about grownups, she told herself, as she went slowly up the stairs to her room. They took everything at face value. Did you have a nice time? Yes, it was very nice. Have fun? It was O.K. But another person her own age would know, just by *looking* at Kathleen, that she had had a perfectly miserable evening, that she was ready to burst into tears of rage and frustration.

When she got into bed and closed her eyes, she could still see Marge and Bruce dancing together, smiling at one another, exchanging whispers and laughter. It wasn't so bad that Marge had maneuvered to have her best friend stuck with an atrocious dancer like Swede, it was just . . . it was just. . . . She rolled over and punched at her pillow, reflecting that she didn't even *like* Marge very well. She was only the girl who lived across the street—no one important. No one at all important.

4

They went up to Blakely, as planned, on the Friday evening train. Kathleen had thought seriously of pleading a nonexistent headache, but she realized that her father would have no difficulty seeing through that fiction.

She took special pains getting ready, and when she came down the stairs, wearing her new print dress and carrying her light coat over her arm, her father nodded approvingly.

"Your mother will be delighted," he said. "You've grown into such a pretty girl."

"I don't see why I can't go too," Wimpy said, for perhaps the thousandth time. Whether his mother came home or not was no longer the issue—Wimpy wanted the train ride. "Why can't I go?"

His father gave him a quick grin. "You weren't invited," he pointed out. "And anyway, someone has to stay here and take care of Alma."

Wimpy looked unsatisfied. "No one has to take care of Alma—*you* know that." He turned and looked at Alma as if to prove his point, and the others looked at her too.

She flushed a little under their steady regard and then came over and put her arm around Wimpy. "You may as well say good-bye to your father and Kathleen and stop grumbling about it. You're stuck with me, young man."

Wimpy sighed. "I guess so. But we *are* going to the movies tonight, don't forget."

"I won't forget," Alma assured him. "How could I? *The Revenge of Dracula* and *Monsters from the Moon,* a double feature."

There were hurried good-byes, and Alma gave Kathleen the box of fruit and cookies she had prepared for them to take on the train. Kathleen's father went back for a last look at the room that had been transformed from the den into a pretty bedroom. They had all had a hand in making the room look lived in. The desk and the other heavy pieces were now in Wimpy's room, and the dark drapes had been replaced by crisp yellow curtains that matched the new bedspread.

"It's a lovely room," Kathleen said, coming to peek across her father's shoulder. "Mother will love it."

"I hope so," he said, in a strange, expressionless voice. Then he glanced at his watch and said that they ought to be getting started.

At the railroad station, Kathleen wandered over to the newsstand and looked at the magazines while her father attended to the tickets and checked through the two small bags. She didn't see anyone she knew, and for this she was vaguely grateful.

Finally they were on the train and pulling out of the station. She was glad that her father didn't expect her to be a gay and sparkling companion. They scarcely exchanged a dozen words during the first hour of the long ride. Her father stared at the magazine he held, not turning the pages, not really seeing the words before him. Kathleen knew, because she was having the same trouble.

She gave up pretending to read after a while and looked out at the flying landscape. It was strange that she and her father could be sitting there side by side and still be so far apart. She knew that they were both thinking of the woman who was waiting for them at the end of the journey; but while Kathleen was thinking about the mother who had brought so much confusion and unhappiness into her early childhood, her father was probably remembering the pretty girl he had fallen in love with, courted, and married.

She turned and studied her father's stern profile for a moment, feeling her heart lurch with pity and love. Without knowing that she was going to do it, she put her hand over his warmly, and when he looked up in surprise, she smiled at him.

"Don't *worry* so much," she said. "It will all work out beautifully."

"I hope so, Kathy." He spoke so heavily that she knew he was remembering the last time he had been sure it would all work out.

"Tell me about Mother," Kathleen said, to lighten the moment. "Tell me what she looked like when you first met her. What you said to her, and what she said to you."

He turned his head and looked at her. "You've heard all that."

"Not lately," she reminded him. "And anyway, talking about her makes her seem more . . . more real."

"What do you remember about her, Kathy?" He asked the question almost as if he dreaded the answer, but Kathleen responded promptly.

"I remember the way she used to sing," she replied. "She had such a pretty voice."

"Yes, she did," her father agreed. "It wasn't ever a great voice, the way her parents insisted. Helen could never have had a musical career, but she had talent. She used to play the piano, too, when I first knew her. Then after we were married, she lost interest in all that."

"Was she really very pretty?" Kathleen asked.

"Very pretty," he said, and then smiled and added, "as a matter of fact, she looked a lot like you. Brown hair and bright blue eyes and a quick smile." A remembering look was in his eyes as he continued. "She laughed a lot in those days—she had the sort of laugh that made everyone smile, even when they didn't see what was so amusing. I remember thinking that she was the happiest person I had ever known." He put his head back against the seat and closed his eyes. "She was like a child in so many ways; she loved to tease people."

Kathleen waited. She wished she dared to say, That was the whole trouble, wasn't it? That she never adjusted to being grown-up and accepting responsibilities—that she never got over being a child. Kathleen had heard a lot of discussion about this over the years, but saying such a thing now would break the spell, and for the moment at least her father was willing to talk about her mother as a person instead of as a patient.

"I remember when Wimpy was a baby and Mother came home from the hospital with him," Kathleen said. "She had a soft pink jacket with feathers; she looked just like a fairy princess."

"I remember that bed jacket, too," her father said. "She always liked frilly things. I expect they made her feel young and frivolous." He dug into his pocket for a cigarette, then just sat there holding it between his fingers, neglecting to light it. "She had a blue silk dress she used to wear to parties. The top was some sort of net stuff that blended with the color of her skin, and from across the room you wondered what was holding the dress up." He grinned at Kathleen. "The gals didn't wear strapless formals in those days. Clothes were expected to have some visible means of support."

Kathleen watched his face and saw that some of the lines of tension had been erased. When he got to his feet and said that he thought he'd go back to the parlor car, she nodded approval. "Fine. I'll just sit here and put on some new fingernail polish. I forgot it when we left home."

They reached Blakely at last and were met at the station by Dr. and Mrs. Lundigan. Both the doctor and his wife were strangers to Kathleen, but they made her feel welcome from the first moment.

"So this is Kathleen," Dr. Lundigan said, as he shook her hand firmly. "I've heard a lot about you."

Kathleen's eyes widened. "You have?"

"I have indeed. Your mother talks about you all the time. She has a whole line-up of pictures of you around the mirror in her room."

"Oh," Kathleen said, a little blankly. "I didn't know about that . . . about the pictures, I mean. I expect they must be pretty out of date."

He shook his head. "Oh no, they're quite recent. You were wearing a formal in one of them."

Mrs. Lundigan took Kathleen by the arm and they followed the two men out to the car. Back at the Lundigans' house they had a light supper, and then Kathleen excused herself and went to her room. She knew that her father and Dr. Lundigan would have a lot to talk about before tomorrow morning.

Before Kathleen went to bed she stood for a long time at the window looking up at the forbidding shadows of the huge building on the hill overlooking the valley. Somewhere behind those darkened windows, her mother was waiting for the morning to come, too. Was she waiting with dread and foreboding, or with serenity and happiness?

Kathleen hadn't expected to sleep well in a strange bed and in an unfamiliar room, but she dropped off almost as soon as her head touched the pillow. When she awakened the room was flooded with sunlight.

Things happened rapidly after that. Kathleen got dressed and went down to breakfast, and then it was time to repack her bag and thank her hostess. They got into Dr. Lundigan's car and drove up to the beautifully tended grounds and through the gates. No one stopped them because Dr. Lundigan's car was familiar to the man on duty.

Kathleen was aware that her palms were moist and her knees were unsteady as she walked into the front entrance between her father and Dr. Lundigan. She had expected to find her mother thin and somehow pitiful, but the woman who was waiting in the big solarium, with her suitcases beside her, was only slightly pale, and she was smiling.

The smile wavered a little when she saw them, and then she got to her feet and extended both hands, one to Kathleen and one to her husband. "Well, hello," she said. "I thought you'd never get here."

Kathleen's father glanced at his watch, and then came over to drop a swift, awkward kiss on his wife's cheek. "It's only ten o'clock, Helen. We didn't want to rush you."

Kathleen came forward woodenly and kissed her mother. She had the feeling that she had been rehearsing for the wrong part in a very bad play. This clear-eyed woman, this stranger, couldn't possibly be the mother Kathleen remembered—the wild-eyed creature who had screamed at them, who had sobbed so unrestrainedly as she had been led away. Kathleen was prepared to pity, to be tolerant, but this woman in the crisp linen dress looked as normal and healthy as anyone.

Kathleen thought of the den at home—that had been so carefully converted into a room for a semi-invalid. The stacks of magazines, the radio within reach of the bed, the blinds that could be easily drawn to blot out the brightness outside. She thought about the new deck chair on the patio, just steps from the bedroom, and the record player that had been moved upstairs, because her mother wouldn't want to listen to all that noise.

"I expect we should be getting started," Kathleen's father was saying briskly. "The train leaves a little before noon and we won't want to rush." He turned to his wife and gave her a reassuring smile. "I'll telephone for a cab while you're saying good-bye to everyone."

"I've already said my good-byes," she told him. "Except for Sam, here." She put her hand on Dr. Lundigan's arm, and he gave her fingers a quick squeeze, smiling down at her as if she were someone very special.

Kathleen's father walked away to call for the taxi.

"Let's go out in the garden for one last time," Kathleen's mother said. When the doctor nodded, she held out her hand to Kathleen, who took it wordlessly and went with them out into the sunshine.

"It's such a lovely place, this garden," Kathleen's mother said. "I'll miss it, Sam."

"Yes, I expect you will," he said sensibly. "You'll miss it until you find something to take its place."

"I'll miss you, too," she told him.

"Only until you realize that you don't need me any more. And that will be very shortly." He looked at Kathleen then and gave her a grin that pulled her into the conversation. "You'll be good to her, won't you, honey? Just until she gets her sea legs back."

It was an odd way of putting it, Kathleen thought, but she answered politely, "Oh yes. I'll take very good care of her, Dr. Lundigan."

At once she knew that she had said the wrong thing. Her mother and the doctor exchanged quick glances before he said, less lightly, "That wasn't exactly what I had in mind. Helen doesn't need taking care of any more—that's why we're letting her go. But she'll need a lot of good friends. I hope you'll be one."

"Of course I will," Kathleen said, and added primly, "I'm her daughter, remember."

Her father came back and they talked about the garden, about the shrubs and the different flowers; it was the conversation of people who were trying to make the time pass quickly.

When the taxi came, Dr. Lundigan walked to the drive with them. He shook hands with all of them, and Kathleen's mother said, "Thank you, Sam. Thank you is an inadequate phrase, but I do mean it."

"Good-bye, Helen. Take care of yourself and let me hear from you once in a while." He held her hand for a second longer than seemed necessary. "You have your home and your family and you are a completely whole person. I know you are going to be very happy."

They got into the taxi that was waiting, and when they pulled away from the hospital, Dr. Lundigan was still standing there looking after them. He waved once, and Kathleen waved in return, but her mother didn't even look back for a final glimpse of the place that had been her home for the better part of nine years.

She looks scared, Kathleen told herself. She looks lost and frightened, as if she'd like to jump out of this cab and run back to where she was secure and cared for. If Kathleen had not felt that her mother was still a stranger, she would have reached over and patted her hand and assured her that everything was going to work out beautifully, the way she had done with her father. Instead, she sat very still and remote in her corner of the cab.

"Well, here we are," Kathleen's father was saying with forced gaiety. "I expect you've already had your breakfast, Helen, but we can have a second breakfast on the train, and after that you can rest for a while before we get home."

"Rest? But I'm not a bit tired. I'm perfectly well, Bob. I thought Dr. Lundigan made that quite clear." She turned her smile from her husband to Kathleen. "Do you think I look like an invalid, Kathy?"

"You look wonderful," Kathleen said, not quite honestly. "As if you could go for a long hike or a ten-mile swim without even stopping to think about it."

Her mother relaxed visibly. "Well, I'm not quite that good yet, but I'm improving. I took up tennis again, and I hadn't played for years and years."

Her husband looked at her gravely. "Tennis?" The way he said it he might just as well have added, at your age? But Kathleen's mother didn't seem to notice.

"Yes. Remember how much we played the

summer before Kathy was born? I was almost as good as you were."

"That was a long time ago," Kathleen's father said. "I haven't played more than a dozen times since. I don't even know where the rackets are any more."

"We'll have to find them and dust them off," his wife said, as if the matter were all settled. Then, feeling the silence, she added more slowly, "Perhaps if you haven't the time, I can persuade Kathy to give me some competition."

"I love tennis," Kathleen said. "But I'm not very good at it."

"We'll improve together," her mother said, and for the first time Kathleen felt a little tug of kinship.

On the train they talked for a while, and then went into the dining car for breakfast. They probably looked like an ordinary family of mother, father, and teen-age daughter, but they did not feel like one. It was difficult to know what to talk about. They were all carefully feeling their way.

"Wimpy wanted to come to meet you, but we talked him into staying at home," Kathy said, to break the silence that was becoming a little strained.

"Wimpy? Oh yes, Greg." She looked across the table at Kathleen with new interest in her eyes. "Why do you call him Wimpy? It seems strange that I've never known about that."

Kathleen glanced at her father for assurance, and then spoke lightly. "When he was real little, about four or five years old, he developed this mad passion for hamburgers—you know, like Wimpy in the Popeye comics—so Father started calling him that and the name stuck. He's been Wimpy ever since."

"Oh, I see." Her mother nodded. "Do they still call him Greg at school?"

"Just the teachers, I guess. The kids all call him Wimpy. And sometimes . . . sometimes Alma calls him Gregory." She was a little hesitant about mentioning Alma, but her mother looked pleased.

"How is Alma? Same old Rock of Gibraltar?"

"Alma doesn't change much." It was Kathleen's father who answered. "She sent her love—did I mention that?"

Kathleen's mother murmured something that passed for assent. Her eyes were abruptly thoughtful, and she picked up her coffee cup, taking a quick sip, before she spoke again. "She's been so faithful about writing and sending me pictures of the children. I still have most of her letters—they were like a breath of home."

"I didn't know that Alma wrote to you," Kathleen said. "I wonder why she never mentioned it. Did you know, Father?" The question caught him off guard, and she saw at once that he had known.

"Almost every week," her mother said. "Sometimes they came while I was having a rather bad time, and they stacked up. Then I had several to read at a time later. The letters usually came on Wednesday, and it got so that I waited for Wednesdays as impatiently as if they were some special holiday."

Kathleen went on eating her breakfast. She was remembering how often Alma had jogged her and Wimpy—yes, and their father, too—to write a little note or send a card, but she had never once said, "If *I* can find the time to write, you should be able to." And all through the years she had kept the woman who hated her in touch with her family through those letters.

"I hope Wimpy didn't make her sit through the second showing of those horror pictures," Kathleen's father said abruptly. Then he added to his wife, "That's how she talked Wimpy into staying at home with her, by taking him to a couple of horror movies."

"She spoils Wimpy," Kathleen volunteered. "She lets him walk all over her."

"She lets all of us walk all over her," Kathleen's father pointed out. "I think she enjoys it."

They finished breakfast and walked back to their car. Kathleen glanced at her watch and saw that there were still two hours to be gotten through before they were home again. What on earth would they find to talk about for two hours?

She looked at the woman by the window and knew a little feeling of panic.

"If you two will excuse me," Kathleen's father said, "I'll go into the club car and have a smoke."

When he had gone, they sat for a moment in awkward silence, and then Kathleen spoke with determined cheerfulness. "The country-side is pretty at this time of year, isn't it?"

"Very beautiful," her mother agreed softly. She turned her head and looked at Kathleen, and then smiled a sad smile, tipping her head back against the seat. "Please don't feel that you have to stay here and entertain me, Kathleen. I'll be quite all right. Maybe I'll take a little nap." She closed her eyes as if she were suddenly very tired, but Kathleen saw that she wasn't relaxed, not really. Her hands were curled into fists and the pulse in her throat leaped unsteadily.

Kathleen settled back. "I'll just stay here," she said comfortably. "Even if you fall asleep, I can watch you and get to know you again." And when her mother opened her eyes in sur-prise, Kathleen nodded matter-of-factly. "I guess we're bound to be strange and stiff at first, but it will wear off."

Her mother reached for her hand and held it tightly for a moment. "Yes," she said. "We are bound to be strangers for a while."

5

T HEY were home at last. Wimpy was out playing baseball, just as if it were an ordinary Saturday, and he came pelting across the street as soon as the car turned into the drive. He stood grinning at his mother as she got out of the car.

"Hello, Wimpy," she said, and leaned forward to kiss his smudged cheek. "I hear you're quite a baseball player."

"Hi," he said, ducking aside from the kiss. Then he added, almost accusingly, "You don't *look* sick."

"I'm not," she said. "Not any more." She started to put her hand out as if she'd like to smooth back his wild hair, and then she changed her mind. "Would you carry one of the bags in for me, Wimpy?"

"Sure," he said, picking up the largest bag and starting for the house.

Alma was waiting on the porch. Kathleen noticed at once that she was wearing a big coverall apron over her pretty jersey dress. She's trying to look like a housekeeper and not a member of the family, Kathleen told herself. She's probably remembering how jealous Mother was before, and this is her way of saying that there's nothing to be jealous about—that she's just the hired help.

"Hello, Mrs. Frazier," Alma said. "You look wonderful."

Kathleen's mother came up the stairs slowly, and when she reached Alma she put her hands out in the friendliest manner possible. "It's good to be home," she said. "And what is all this Mrs. Frazier nonsense? I'm Helen, remember?"

"Of course I remember," Alma replied. She looked at Wimpy and said, "Greg Frazier, you promised you'd wash up and comb your hair before your mother got here."

"The bases were loaded," Wimpy explained glibly. "I couldn't leave with the bases loaded, could I?"

"Take your mother's suitcase into her room, Wimpy," his father directed, and shifted the bags he was carrying a trifle impatiently. "We

68

don't have to stand here on the porch all afternoon."

Wimpy headed the procession into the house and carried his mother's suitcase to the room that had been prepared for her. "This used to be the den, but now it's your room," he told his mother importantly. "I helped paint the walls. I did that wall all by myself, didn't I, Alma?"

Alma didn't answer at once; she was looking at the closed expression on Mrs. Frazier's face. "You don't like it," she said anxiously. "I was so sure that yellow was your favorite color."

"It's very nice," Kathleen's mother said. "And yellow is still my favorite color." She stood in the doorway looking around as if she were inspecting a room for rent. She moved aside to let her husband come in with the other suitcase, but didn't quite look at him as she continued, "At the hospital most of the rooms are painted in tones of lavender. It's supposed to be a soothing color—nothing that will excite the patients in case they happen to be extremely color conscious." She looked around at all of them then, and found a quick smile to go with the polite words. "Anyway—it's a lovely room and I do thank you, all of you."

"You'll probably want to change into something more comfortable," Kathleen's father said. "We'll clear out and let you get squared away. O.K.?"

"O.K.," she said quietly.

"Well, you heard your mother. Clear out, you two!" He came over and kissed his wife, who was still standing beside the door looking as if she hadn't yet made up her mind to stay. "Just take it easy, Helen," he said, as if she were a very small child in need of comfort and reassurance. "Kathleen or Alma will help you unpack your things when you're ready." He shepherded them all out into the hall and closed the door softly.

Wimpy immediately took off for the kitchen to raid the refrigerator, and Kathleen went upstairs to put her things away. When she came back down a few minutes later, she found her father and Alma in the hallway beside the telephone, checking the mail and the phone calls and things that had come up during his absence.

"Mr. Crenshaw called twice," Alma was saying, "last night and then again this morning. I took the number, but he didn't want to leave a message."

"I'll give him a call," Kathleen's father said. "Anything else?"

Alma bit her lip thoughtfully, and then shook her head. "Nothing important," she said.

"In other words, nothing that you can't handle." He smiled as he said the words and put the mail back on the hall table. "Come on. What happened?"

She shrugged. "Well, if you must know, the dogcatcher picked up Chipper. He got out of the yard late yesterday afternoon, and we looked for him half the night. Wimpy was almost frantic. Then the first thing this morning we called the Humane Society and, sure enough, they'd picked him up. So we went right down and got him. Mr. Larkin drove us downtown. The fine wasn't very much—just five dollars."

"It'll come out of Wimpy's allowance," his father said firmly. "How many times do you have to tell that kid about keeping the gate latched?"

"It didn't have to be Wimpy," Alma pointed out. "A lot of the other boys go in and out through that gate. And, anyway, Wimpy was punished enough by all the worry he had—not to mention having to miss that horror show while he was out searching for his dog."

Abruptly Mr. Frazier laughed. "Alma, are you sure you didn't *bribe* the dogcatcher to pick up Chipper?"

They're like a mother and father, Kathleen thought, coming the rest of the way down the stairs. Fussing over their children, arguing a little—and then dissolving all the differences with laughter.

They went out into the kitchen where Alma

71

had the coffeepot plugged in, and Alma poured two cups while Kathleen helped herself to a Coke from the refrigerator. It was almost like any other Saturday—the three of them taking a coffee break and talking of inconsequential things. Almost, but not quite. For slowly encircling them, as relentlessly as a cold wind blowing through the warm and comfortable rooms, was the feeling of an alien presence, a stranger in the house.

"Perhaps your mother would like a cup of tea," her father suggested when Kathleen got up to refill the coffee cups. "Why don't you ask her?"

A quiet voice spoke from the doorway. "I smelled the coffee and it lured me out. I'd like it much more than the tea."

Kathleen's father got to his feet hastily. As if she were a visitor, Kathy thought, as if she were someone he had to be polite to.

"I'll pour it for you," Kathleen said, but her mother shook her head.

"No. I can wait on myself."

She opened the wrong cupboard the first time, but the next time she found the cup and poured her coffee and came to the table. Kathy slid over on the bench to make room for her. She was sorry for her mother without quite knowing why.

There was the sound of running feet on the

walk and up the back steps, and then Marge's unmistakable knock on the screen door.

"Come on in, Margie," Kathleen called, and when her friend bounded into the kitchen, she waved the Coke bottle invitingly. "Help yourself to a Coke and say hello to Mother. Mother, this is Marge Chessman. She lives right across the street." The words slipped out so easily and naturally that she was scarcely conscious of having said them. *Mother.* For the first time she hadn't hesitated over the word.

"Hi," Marge said, in the shy, little-girl tone she reserved for grownups. "I'm so glad to meet you at last, Mrs. Frazier."

"I feel as if I know you already," Kathleen's mother said. "Alma sent me some snapshots of you and Kathy taken on a picnic last summer. You both looked as though you were having such a good time."

"We always have a good time," Marge said. "And that reminds me of why I really came over. Some of the kids are planning a beach party down near the Point tonight. Swede's got his father's station wagon and some of the mothers made salads and baked beans and stuff, and all the rest of us are going to bring hot dogs and marshmallows and potato chips. It'll be a real ball."

Kathleen looked around the circle of faces, and then shook her head. "Well, I couldn't go

73

tonight. Not on Mother's first night home."
Automatically she looked at Alma to back her
up, but Alma's face was carefully expressionless. Kathy looked at her father, and then at her
mother sitting quietly beside her. "There'll be
other beach parties later on," she said.

Marge pouted prettily. "But, Kathy, it won't
be any fun if you aren't there! I'm sure your
mother wouldn't mind. Would you, Mrs. Frazier?"

"No, of course I wouldn't mind. You mustn't
think of staying home on my account, Kathy.
I'm not a guest, you know. I'll be around for a
long, long time."

Kathleen swallowed. "Honestly, Mother, I'd
just as soon stay home."

"But I would much prefer that you went to
the party with your friends," her mother said.
"I don't want to be treated like company."

"There! It's all settled," Marge said triumphantly. "Thanks a million, Mrs. Frazier. I'll
run back home and call some of the other kids.
We'll leave around six-thirty, Kathy. You can
run out when you see the station wagon in
front of my house. It's pink—isn't that a panic?
Wouldn't you just know that Swede would
drive a pink station wagon?"

When Marge had gone, Kathleen excused
herself and went up to her room to decide what
she would wear to the beach party. Most of her

things were in the clothes hamper and there wouldn't be time to wash and iron them before evening. She thought nostalgically of the days, not too far back, when Alma took care of such minor problems. Clean clothes had appeared in her closet and in her bureau drawers as if by magic. But Alma said that she was old enough now to take care of her own personal belongings.

There were some clean jeans in her bottom drawer and several men's shirts which weren't very glamorous, but were suitable for the beach. She took her bathing suit, too, just in case someone wanted to go for a swim. It was really too cold for swimming, but you never could tell. Someone—someone like Bruce—might suggest a midnight swim, and she probably would be the only one brave enough to go into the icy water. She held the bathing suit up to herself and turned slowly before the mirror. She thought ahead to the evening, and of Bruce saying things like, "You're such a good sport, Kathy. I guess I've been looking for a girl like you." And she could see the two of them swimming easily side by side. She turned up her radio and started putting rollers in her hair.

Someone came galloping up the stairs, and then Wimpy appeared in the doorway, scowling at her. "I've been yelling at you," he announced coldly. "Some dizzy girl is on the phone. She wants to talk to you."

Kathleen followed him down the stairs, ignoring his comments on people who had their radios blaring so loud that they couldn't hear a jet bomber in the next room.

It was a girl Kathleen didn't know very well, who was going to the beach party. Her name was Linda Jo, and she wanted to find out what Kathleen was wearing, and whether they should take sweaters in case it turned cold, and what about bathing suits.

"I honestly don't know," Kathleen admitted. "I was only invited myself a few minutes ago. I'm going to wear jeans and a shirt, but I'm taking my bathing suit along just in case."

"Oh," Linda Jo said. "Well, I'm thinking about wearing my new beachcomber outfit. It's a violent pink shade and it makes my sun tan look wonderful, but if the rest of the girls are going to wear jeans. . . ."

"I don't know what the others are wearing," Kathleen said. "*I'm* wearing jeans."

"I'll call Margie and see what she thinks," Linda Jo said. Then she added, "I hear your mother is back. I was so *surprised*."

"You were?" Kathleen said politely. "Why?"

"I don't know, except that it's so—so unusual after all these years and years. I mean . . . well, I always thought that cases like that. . . ." She

76

floundered a little. "I just took it for granted that she was gone permanently."

"Apparently not," Kathleen said, hating the sharp note in her voice, but unable to do anything about it. She disliked people who pried for information about things that were none of their concern.

"Well. I'll see you tonight then," Linda Jo said uncertainly. "So long, Kathleen."

Kathleen stood there for a moment and then hung up the phone softly. There wasn't really any reason to be mad at Linda Jo, who was just trying to be friendly and interested. She was going to have to get used to these questions and learn not to be quite so thin-skinned.

The door to her mother's bedroom was ajar and Kathleen could hear her moving about, opening and closing doors and drawers. Kathleen knocked lightly. "May I come in?"

"Yes, of course," her mother answered, and looked up with a warm smile when Kathleen entered. "I'm just getting some of my things put away. I—I noticed that your father had brought down some of my old hatboxes and I couldn't resist opening them."

She looked around and made a distracted gesture toward the dresses that had been unfolded and placed across the bottom of the bed. "All my things seem to be hopelessly out-of-date. You'll have to go shopping with me for some spring and summer clothes."

"I'd like that," Kathleen said. She got some hangers from the closet and started hanging up the dresses. She lined up the shoes in a corner of the closet and shook out the folds from a bathrobe that would have been more suitable for someone her own age.

"Can I do anything else?" she asked, when all the clothes were hung away.

"There are some magazines on the chair," her mother said. "You might put them in the magazine rack in the living room. They're fairly recent issues."

Kathleen picked up the magazines. They were all the type that were popular with the girls in her age group—young fashions and teenage problems about dating and choosing the right career. Her heart sank as she turned the pages. If it were true that her mother's trouble had been her inability to accept maturity, these magazines certainly gave no indication that she had overcome the problem. Nevertheless, Kathleen took them in the living room and placed them in the rack with the others.

When she went back to the bedroom, her mother was trying on hats. She confessed to Kathleen that she had always been mad about hats and bought a new one for every possible occasion. "I remember when I joined the P.T.A.

when you were in the first grade," she told her daughter. "I was determined to go to every meeting and never wear the same hat twice."

"Why?" Kathleen asked.

Her mother adjusted a flowered confection to her liking, and then turned her head this way and that to admire it. "I really don't know why," she confessed, "except that there seemed to be a certain prestige in wearing a different hat each month."

It was like talking to someone her own age, Kathleen found herself thinking. She couldn't remotely imagine bringing her problems to this woman, the way she could to Alma. She couldn't imagine saying, "Mother, I don't really want to go to this beach party tonight. You see, there's this boy—"

So she said nothing at all about the beach party, or about Bruce, or about Swede, who always went out of his way to speak to her since that evening at Marge's when she had danced with him. She had the awful conviction that Swede was beginning to think of her, in his curious uncomplicated way, as his girl, and she couldn't think of anything less appealing.

"You're so quiet," her mother said at last. "I have the feeling that you aren't too happy about this beach party tonight. If I talked out of turn when I accepted for you, I'm truly sorry."

Kathleen looked at her sharply. It was unnerving that she should be able to read her thoughts so accurately. Perhaps a mother's intuition *was* something special. "It's funny you should say that," she admitted, "because I really wasn't sold on the idea at first, but now I'm glad I let Marge talk me into it."

Everything was put away at last. "I'll run along now," Kathleen said, "and see about helping Alma with dinner."

"I could help, too," her mother suggested. "I'm a little rusty, but I'll get back into the swing of things before too long."

"Of course you will," Kathleen said. "But it's been a long day for you. Why not take a rest before dinner?" She watched the brightness fade from her mother's eyes and knew that she had said the wrong thing. She had to remember that her mother wasn't a convalescent.

Kathleen went out into the kitchen where Alma was making a salad. Their eyes met gravely, and she answered the unspoken question. "Mother's resting before dinner. I helped her put her things away."

Alma nodded. "That's nice, sweetie. Now, how about setting the table on the patio. I thought we might eat out there."

"Good idea," Kathleen said, but made no move to get the dishes from the cupboard. "Alma? How come I never knew that you were writing to Mother all the time she was in that place?"

Alma looked at her. "You never asked."

"It was a wonderful thing for you to do," Kathleen said soberly. "A wonderful, thoughtful thing to do."

Alma grinned, her old easy grin. "Well, now, honey, we don't have to get sticky about it, do we?"

Kathleen grinned back at her, but her voice when she spoke was just a little unsteady. "Just the same—even if it does sound sticky—you're very nice, Alma. No wonder all of us. . . ." She hesitated over the word *love* and concluded, a trifle inadequately, "No wonder all of us are so—so fond of you."

6

As KATHLEEN had feared, she was Swede's date at the beach party. At any rate, he had saved a place for her in the front seat beside him. Bruce and Marge were in the back with half a dozen other young people. When they had picked up everyone, there were too many jammed into the pink station wagon, all of them boys and girls Kathleen had seen before. Some of them she didn't know by name, but no one got around to introductions.

They drove out to the Point, laughing, singing, and calling good-natured insults back and forth. It was the first time Kathleen had ever been included in such a group, although Marge had been invited to these outings all during the past year. She found that she was having a very good time, and when Swede grinned down at her and asked if she were having fun, she nodded enthusiastically.

The picnic things were unloaded from the back of the station wagon and carried down to the beach, and then, while the boys started the beach fire, the girls assembled the food. Someone had an accordion farther down the beach, and the strains of the music almost drowned out the sounds coming from Bruce's transistor radio. Finally they turned the radio off and listened to the boy play his accordion.

"I've got a wonderful idea," Linda Jo announced. "Why don't we ask them to join us? There seem to be just the two of them, and we have plenty of food. They look lonesome all by themselves."

Bruce took her hand and spoke in a solemn voice, as if he were explaining something to a very young child. "Dear one," he said, "they probably *want* to be lonesome."

After a while the two with the accordion moved farther down the beach, and they turned the radio on again. One of the couples started dancing in the sand, barefoot, and announced that it was fun. Swede took Kathleen's hand and they started to dance with the others. On the beach they all looked funny and awkward, and it didn't matter what a terrible dancer Swede was.

Darkness started to fall as they milled around the fire, dancing and singing snatches of songs. The waves slapped at the beach, marking a rhythmic underbeat to the music.

"I'm dying of hunger," one of the boys said finally, and collapsed on the beach to prove it.

The fire had turned to glowing coals, perfect for roasting hot dogs and marshmallows. Everyone helped.

Kathleen had thought she wasn't hungry, but the food, heaped on paper plates, tasted marvelous. She watched in complete fascination while Swede put away seven hot dogs in rapid succession. He also consumed quantities of potato salad, baked beans, Coke, and cake.

"I'm a growing boy," he told Kathleen complacently, when he caught her amused eyes watching him.

"You'll be growing in the wrong direction if you always eat like *that*," she warned him, and he laughed and laughed as if she had said something terribly witty.

It was just too bad, she found herself thinking, that it was so easy to charm someone you didn't care about charming. She glanced across the fire to where Bruce and Marge were whispering and laughing together, but neither of them was paying any attention to her.

Someone suggested that the beach fire was going out and that they should get more wood. As if the words were a signal, couples started drifting away from the circle of light, until finally just Swede and Kathleen were left beside the dying fire.

"We can burn up all these paper plates and empty paper bags," Kathleen said. "That should keep the fire going until someone gets back with some wood." She started gathering up the soggy plates and potato-chip bags, and feeding them, one by one, to the fire. After a moment Swede helped her, and when they had the fire going again, he went off into the shadows and came back with an armload of driftwood, which he piled carefully around the flames. Kathleen gathered up all the silver and cups and the remains of the picnic supper. "I suppose we might as well pack this stuff," she suggested. Swede nodded cheerfully and helped her pile everything back into the boxes. There were a few marshmallows left and she offered them to Swede, but he shook his head.

"Nope, I don't want to get fat," he said solemnly.

He carried the boxes up and put them in the back of the station wagon. The fire was burning down again when he came back, but he found a stick and stirred up the coals. Together they watched the sparks fly off into the darkness.

"They look like a swarm of fireflies," Kathleen said, and he nodded.

"Yep. Nothing is quite as fascinating as a fire." He was squatting beside the campfire, but now he sank back on the sand and rested on one elbow. "You look sort of spooky standing there with the firelight flickering across your face and your hair all wild."

She reached up automatically to smooth her hair, and then looked over her shoulder, peering hopefully into the darkness. "It's certainly taking them a long time to find wood," she said, and then as she saw Swede's grin, she felt her cheeks burn. "Well, it *is* taking them a long time," she repeated stubbornly. "It must be getting awfully late."

"It is, at that," Swede said, and put two fingers into his mouth and whistled—a whistle that made her jump and that probably carried for miles along the beach.

Almost at once the others started straggling back, two by two and hand in hand. Some of them brought wood, but most of them had forgotten. They sat around the fire while the last of it burned, and then someone said they'd better put it out and start home. They carried seawater to the fire in used cans, and drenched it. Swede scattered the coals and they kicked sand up over the ashes until the cheerful circle of light was entirely blotted up in the darkness. Kathleen tipped back her head and looked at the stars, which seemed far away and very cold.

They weren't so noisy driving home. No one seemed interested in singing the school songs. Swede delivered all of the others before driving Bruce and Marge and Kathleen home. It was much later than Kathleen was supposed to be out and she wondered, nervously, whether her father would be cross.

She got out of the car with Marge and told Swede hurriedly that he didn't have to come up to the door with her, that she'd had a lovely time, thank you, and good night. Bruce, who had swung himself into the front seat beside Swede, gave both the girls the benefit of his lazy grin.

"So long, dolls. See you around."

She whispered a hasty good night to Marge and ran across the street and up the walk before the station wagon had driven off. She let herself into the house, and her father, who was reading one of his technical journals, looked up with a faint frown.

"I know it's awfully late," Kathy said. "We were having so much fun that no one thought about the time."

"I see." He put aside the magazine without even marking the page, and Kathleen realized that he hadn't been reading it at all—just staring at the print, waiting for her to come home. "Well, I suppose we can extend the curfew on Saturday evenings. You're a young woman now, practically seventeen."

"Alma says that on special occasions like this —parties, and dances, and things—it's O.K., because after all, when you go in someone else's car, you can't come home whenever you feel like it."

His face darkened a little. "We'll have a family council one of these days and work out some new house rules. In the meantime, Kathleen, I think it might be a good idea if you came to *me* about these things." He paused, and then added, "Or to your mother."

She stared at him and swallowed and said nothing, and when he gave the little nod that meant she was dismissed, she whispered good night and tiptoed up the stairs. It wasn't fair, she told herself, as she undressed in the darkness and slipped into bed. It wasn't one bit fair that for years and years he had turned her problems aside by suggesting that she ask Alma. Now, all of a sudden, he expected her to forget all that, and come running to him.

She knew it was because her mother was home again. Her return was bound to change everything that was normal and accepted in her life. Kathleen was sorry for her mother and she was glad that she wasn't ill any more, that she no longer had to be confined in a sanatorium, however comfortable. But just the same, she couldn't dismiss the feeling of resentment.

Normally it was Alma who waited up for her, Alma who would ask how she had enjoyed herself, and who was there, and what they had eaten. She knew again the faint nostalgic sense of loss as she turned her cheek against the pillow, closed her eyes, and finally slept.

It was morning.

Kathleen opened her eyes and stretched and yawned, wondering what there was about this day that made her feel different—not relaxed and peaceful the way she usually felt on a Sunday morning, but as though something might be going to happen. She could hear noises downstairs as she dressed, muted sounds unlike the usual happy clamor that typified the day. The radio was turned low, and the soft tinkle of glass and silver meant that Alma was setting the table in the dining room.

Kathleen flew down the stairs a few minutes later and out into the kitchen. Alma was just finishing the breakfast preparations, but she was dressed for church. She even had her hat on.

"Oh, there you are," she said brightly, when she saw Kathleen. "Just in time to take over. I'm off to church." She untied her apron and slipped it off as she was speaking. "The sausages are in the oven, the coffee's perked, and the peaches are chilling in the refrigerator. All you have to do is fry the eggs and then dish up. You can make toast at the table. Wimpy is plugging in the toaster and finishing setting the table."

"Aren't you going to have breakfast with us?"

"There isn't time. I'll have to rush as it is. And Susan Malone is picking me up right after church to spend the day with her. You *will* remember to put the ham in the oven as soon as you're back from church?"

"Yes, I'll remember," Kathleen said, and added slowly, "I hope you'll have a nice day with Mrs. Malone; you haven't visited her in ages, have you?"

"Ages," Alma agreed, and then asked, "how was the beach party last night? Gay, mad fun?"

"It was O.K.," Kathleen said.

Her father came out into the kitchen and asked politely whether he might drive Alma to church, but she said no, thank you, the walk would be good for her.

They were all very courteous to one another, not a bit like a family.

Wimpy and his mother were in the living room reading the Sunday papers when Kathleen called them for breakfast. As usual, Wimpy was buried in the sports page and protested at being interrupted.

"Breakfast is being served right *now*, young man," his father said in a firm, no-nonsense tone. "March!"

"There ought to be something I can do to help," Kathleen's mother said, but Kathy shook her head.

"Oh no, you just sit down here at the foot of the table and pour the coffee. Wimpy will bring in the percolator right away."

She dished up everything and trotted back and forth with the platters, but she had forgotten about the hot pads and had to stand, shifting a hot plate from hand to hand, while Wimpy and her father looked for them in the sideboard. The coffee cooled before it was time for a second cup, because no one remembered to plug in the percolator again, and the toast was ready before they were ready for *it*.

Kathleen was beginning to feel rushed and irritated long before the meal was over. Alma made everything look so easy, but she had to keep jumping up for things like salt, napkins, and milk for her mother's coffee. The rest of them drank their coffee black.

Her mother sat serenely in her place at the end of the table, making polite conversation, eating very little, and watching them, one after another, as though they were strange equations she was trying to work out.

"What would you like to do today?" Kathleen's father asked her, and she looked at him gravely.

"I really have no ideas, Bob. Just . . . getting acquainted with my family again."

"I have to put in the ham as soon as we're back from church," Kathleen volunteered. "We can plan on eating again around four, if that's all right with everyone."

"I have a much better suggestion," her father said. "Let's forget about the ham. We can go for a long drive and stop somewhere for dinner. How about it, Wimpy?" He turned to his son and Wimpy nodded. He looked to his wife for a smile of approval, and then at Kathleen. "How about you, Chick? You aren't going to object, are you?"

"Not me," Kathleen assured him. "The last time Alma trusted me with a Sunday dinner, I had an awful time making things come out even. The vegetables were ready before the meat was cooked, and the gravy burned while I was carving the roast, and I forgot about the salad until—" Suddenly she broke off in dismay and exclaimed, "The peaches! Alma put the peaches in the freezer to chill and I forgot all about them." She pushed back her chair and ran into the kitchen to rescue the peaches, which had started to freeze.

Then Kathleen went back to the dining room to gather up the dishes. Everyone wanted to help, and they got in each other's way until she was ready to scream. Alma managed things so efficiently that you never even thought about it. A dishwasher simply did away with the problem of dishes. You never remembered that they had to be picked up and stacked in the machine, that the food had to be put away and the table cleared.

It was a rush getting ready for church, but at last they were on their way. Kathleen's mother and father sat in the front seat, and Kathleen sat in the back with Wimpy. Usually she rode in the front beside her father, and Alma shared the back seat with Wimpy—it was just another of the changes they would have to make.

Kathleen knew that necks craned and heads turned as the family went down the aisle at church, but she kept her eyes steadfastly ahead and tried to ignore the little stir that followed them like a small wave.

It was hard to concentrate on the sermon with her mother sitting straight and still beside her. She looked at Wimpy, on the other side, and noticed that his cowlick was pushing up through his careful brushing. Alma was the only one who could do anything with that cowlick of Wimpy's.

The entire day was uncomfortable and somehow tense. Wimpy got bored with the long drive and complained about missing his baseball practice. Kathleen had a headache and she had forgotten her sunglasses. The place they finally stopped for dinner was not a happy choice. Outside it looked rustic and interesting, but the dining room was heavy with stale odors, and the food was greasy and unappetizing.

"We should have gone back to the hotel in town," Kathleen's father grumbled, as he struggled with a tough steak. "It's not much for atmosphere, but at least you can put a fork in the gravy."

Wimpy, who had been dissuaded from ordering a hamburger, ate glumly.

Keeping the conversation going was such uphill work that Kathleen's father finally gave Wimpy a quarter to play the jukebox, and they finished their meal to the blatant accompaniment of hillbilly music.

They were all quiet in the car driving home. Then, after a long stretch of silence, Kathleen's mother said, "I see something blue."

Without even thinking about it, Kathy said, "The sky. That big patch of blue over there."

Her mother turned around and smiled at her. "No, not the sky."

"Your scarf, then,"

"No, it's nothing in the car."

"Oh. Well then, the wild flowers. The blue ones growing in the fields."

"That's right. Now it's your turn."

Wimpy scowled at them. "Hey, what goes on?"

"It's a game we used to play when I was little," Kathleen explained. "I haven't thought about it for years and years."

"I want to play, too," Wimpy said.

They played the silly little game the rest of the way home, and when they got out of the car, Kathleen felt closer to her mother than she would have believed possible. It was as if in some way they had reached into the shadowy past and pulled out a happy memory to draw them together.

"If I change my good clothes, can I go play baseball now?" Wimpy demanded, before they were scarcely in the house again. Kathleen started to answer, and then realized that the question wasn't addressed to her, but to her mother. Mr. Frazier was putting the car away in the garage.

Mrs. Frazier looked startled for just a moment, and then she answered carefully, "It's fine with me, dear. But be sure to change your good shoes."

He grinned at her, as if he found her ignorance endearing. "Hey, I couldn't play baseball in these shoes even if I wanted to. I wear track shoes. I got a pair for my birthday. They're real keen. I'll show you."

When he clattered down the stairs a few minutes later, Kathleen was making lemonade to take out on the patio, and Mr. Frazier was clumsily unloading the dishwasher.

"You look funny working in the kitchen," Wimpy told him. "How come you don't let Mother do stuff like this, if she isn't sick any more?"

His father looked at him unsmilingly. "Maybe I like to help. Ever think of that?"

"You never helped Alma," Wimpy pointed out. He went out on the patio where his mother was sitting in the lounge chair, and showed her the track shoes.

"They look very professional," she told him gravely. "I'd like to come and watch you play some time."

"Come on now," Wimpy invited. "It isn't a regular Little League game, just practice. Of course, you'd have to sit on the ground, because there aren't any bleachers."

She gave him a quick smile, and then looked past him at Kathleen, who had just carried out the pitcher of lemonade and the glasses. "Perhaps another time would be better, Wimpy," she said. "I seem to be a little dressed up for sitting on the ground."

7

THE next week was one that Kathleen had dreaded, but it passed almost uneventfully.

Alma was there as always. Kathleen and Wimpy went off to school each day and their father to work, just as usual. Their mother's bedroom door was always closed when they left the house, and when they returned home, she was usually sitting on the patio lounge, reading or knitting or just looking off into the distance as if her thoughts were a million miles away.

The days settled into a pattern, but not the familiar pattern, because there was someone else in the house—moving through the familiar rooms, making her presence felt in a hundred ways.

People started calling her mother on the telephone and dropping in to visit her. Some of them managed to act as if she had simply been away on a trip. In some ways this attitude was even harder to cope with than that of the frankly curious acquaintances, who wanted to know all about her "treatment" and her astonishing "cure."

One of the most persistent of these, an old school friend of Kathleen's mother named Mrs. Milburn, had a most upsetting effect on the entire household. She arrived one evening after they had finished dinner. Wimpy and Kathleen were busy with their homework at the kitchen table, Alma was putting dishes in the dishwasher, and Mr. and Mrs. Frazier were sitting out on the patio. They were talking about the best kind of shrubs to put in the rockery when a strange car whirled into the driveway. A large, overdressed woman got out of the car and swooped down on them.

Her opening remark set the tone for the entire visit. "Helen, my poor dear, how utterly wonderful to see you again," she said loudly. "But you're so *thin*. What did they do to you in that dreadful place?"

Kathleen's father made his escape almost immediately with a murmured excuse about some figures he had to check on. He hurried through the kitchen and into the living room, and Kathleen heard the door bang behind him.

Unfortunately, Mrs. Milburn had a voice that carried, and she asked questions that were painful to Kathleen's mother and embarrassing to the rest of them. She wanted to know whether Helen had ever been put in a straitjacket, and whether any of the patients ever became violent and harmed a member of the staff. Was it true that they weren't allowed to use knives and forks because they might injure themselves? And did all the meals served at the hospital taste alike because of the generous portions of sedatives that went into them?

The kitchen windows as well as the patio doors were standing open. Kathleen and Wimpy, working at the kitchen table, could scarcely avoid overhearing the whole conversation. Alma must have heard, too, though she gave no indication. She calmly made a pitcher of iced coffee and carried it out to the patio.

Kathleen heard her mother say, "Why, thank you, Alma," in a surprised little voice. She added, "You know Virginia Milburn, don't you?"

Alma murmured something that sounded polite, but Mrs. Milburn only said, "We've met," in a tone that was suddenly frosty, and almost before Alma was back in the house, she started again.

"Now, Helen, don't tell me you're still keeping *her* around here after all the trouble she made last time? I just wouldn't put up with it if I were you. I'd tell Bob Frazier once and for all—"

Kathleen's mother broke into the tirade to explain that it wasn't like that at all, that Alma was a very good friend.

Wimpy looked across the table at Kathleen, who had paused with her pen in mid-air. His brows were drawn together into frowning bumps, and his whisper was almost loud enough to carry through the open window. "What's the matter with that silly old woman, anyway? Why doesn't Mother tell her to keep quiet or go home?"

Kathleen waved him to silence. Their mother was speaking so softly that it was an effort to hear.

". . . she wrote to me regularly all the time I was away. None of my other friends bothered."

"Well!" Mrs. Milburn managed to sound hurt and indignant at the same time. "Well, maybe I didn't write to you, Helen, but at least I wasn't trying to snatch your husband from behind your back."

"That's pretty silly," Kathleen's mother said. "Alma is my friend."

"A fine friend," the woman repeated scornfully. "I suppose you realize that it's been town talk for years and years. The way she's *burrowed* her way into this family, going to P.T.A. meetings and serving on the lunchroom committees, and taking on all the rights and privileges of a mother."

"Privileges?" There was a smile in her mother's carefully chosen words. "Unless my memory fails me, there were always too many mothers who turned their backs on such privileges. I'm sure that Kathleen and Wimpy appreciated her interest."

"Kathleen and Wimpy are just children—they can't see through her the way adults can."

Kathleen got up and banged her books together. "I guess I'll go up to my room to study," she said in a loud, clear voice. "It's so noisy around here you can't hear yourself think."

Wimpy looked at her round-eyed, but her rudeness had the desired effect, and almost at once Mrs. Milburn left.

It was later that same week that two of the girls at school attached themselves to Kathleen when she was starting home, and announced that they were coming with her.

"Linda Jo was telling us that you have some old records that would be perfect for our pantomimes," they explained. "You don't mind, do you, Kathleen?"

Kathleen hesitated only a second. "No, of course I don't mind. We . . . we won't be able to make a lot of racket, though."

The girls nodded understandingly, and one of them linked her arm through Kathleen's. "Because of your mother—we know. And we'll be quiet as field mice, honest."

"It isn't that," Kathleen said a little stiffly. "It's just—well, I haven't brought anyone around because we thought she should have time to get used to *us* before we start herding a lot of outsiders through the house—" She broke off at the girl's quick grin. "I'm sorry, that didn't sound very hospitable, did it?"

"Not very. But never mind, my skin is nice and thick. How about yours, Jenny?"

Jenny felt her arm gravely. "Pretty thick. I'll chance it."

Any other afternoon Kathleen's mother would have been sitting quietly on the patio, reading a book. But today she was seated at the kitchen table, making hats. The entire table was strewn with old hat crowns, bits of lace and ribbon, and artificial flowers. There was also a great deal of veiling and something that looked like chicken wire.

Kathleen, who had ushered her guests into the house ahead of her, paused just inside the door. Her mother looked up with a quick, warm smile. "Oh hi," she said. "I'm sorry everything's such a mess. I'm making a hat."

Kathleen nodded. "Mother, this is Jenny Norton and Pat Rawley. They came to see about borrowing some of my records." She looked around, then added, "Where's Alma?"

"She went down to meet a friend of hers who was passing through town. I told her I could manage dinner."

"Fine," Kathleen said briefly. "I'll help."

She led the girls into the hallway and upstairs to her room, and she could feel the glances they exchanged behind her back.

"Your mother looks very well," Jenny said, to break the uncomfortable silence.

"She's fine now," Kathleen said briefly, and brought out the record albums with more haste than was absolutely necessary.

"You look like her," Pat said, and then turned away from Kathleen quickly, as though she had said something unforgivably tactless.

When they had selected the records for the pantomime, Kathleen led the girls down the stairs again and let them out the front door. Her mother looked up when she came back into the kitchen.

"Your friends left?" she asked. "Oh, too bad. I wanted to show them the finished product. Look, isn't it cute?"

Kathleen stared at the hat. "What . . . what is it?"

"It's a hat to wear to the Mother-Daughter Breakfast next Saturday morning. We had our invitation just a few days ago, remember?"

"I . . . I didn't realize that you'd want to go," Kathleen said. She took the hat in her hands and turned it slowly. "It's certainly different."

"You don't like it," her mother said at once, and some of the brightness went out of her face. Then she smiled again. "Never mind, I'll just wear a regular hat and not enter the contest at all."

Kathleen said nothing. She hadn't been thinking about the hat contest. Every year at the Mother-Daughter Breakfast there were prizes for the prettiest hat, the funniest hat, and the most unusual hat. But a girl didn't want her mother making a spectacle of herself before the entire school, especially if she had a mother people would be watching for any hint of . . . of peculiarity. Couldn't her mother see that?

Her mother was watching her gravely. "Don't you want to go to the breakfast, Kathleen? Is that it?"

"Oh yes. Of course I want to go. I wouldn't miss it. It's just . . . well. . . ."

Her mother nodded. "Other years you've taken Alma."

Kathleen swallowed. "Well, yes—but that

doesn't make any difference. I'm sure Alma won't mind not going this year." She put the hat down slowly, still not looking at her mother. "It's an awfully cute hat," she finished flatly.

It was a cute hat. Fanciful, but cute. The small crown was crowded with flowers in every possible hue, and the wide brim was penned in with fine chicken wire to make a run for half a dozen velvety yellow chicks.

"I borrowed the chicks from one of your old Easter baskets," Kathleen's mother said, and then went on doggedly. "Would anyone think it odd if . . . if the *three* of us came to the breakfast?"

Kathleen thought about it for a moment. "No, of course they wouldn't think it was odd. A lot of girls bring grandmothers and aunts and godmothers. I can make reservations for the three of us."

Her mother started to gather up all the odds and ends of material and stuff them back into a shopping bag. "Fine," she said, as if it were all settled. "Will you run down and put this wire on your father's workbench, Kathleen? It's time to put in the potatoes and meat loaf."

"Don't forget the Mother-Daughter Breakfast next Saturday," Kathleen reminded Alma the next day. "Dad will drive us down before his golf date, and we can take a taxi home."

Alma, who was pouring fruit juice into the glasses, looked up in surprise. "But, Kathleen. Your mother—"

"Oh, she's going, too," Kathleen said. "Several of the girls bring grandmothers or favorite aunts, you know. It really doesn't make any difference, just so they know how many to prepare for, so I'll put us down for three."

Alma nodded. "That might be a good idea," she said, as if she were thinking out loud. "Seeing the three of us together would help clear up any . . . misunderstandings."

But on Saturday, at the last moment, Kathleen's mother decided not to go. She said she had a blinding headache, and she didn't even get out of bed. Marge and her mother came over to ride down with them. It had been planned during the week that Kathleen's father would drive them down, and Mr. Chessman would pick them up after the breakfast. Mrs. Chessman looked especially pretty in a new blue suit that had been purchased for the occasion; and for the moment, at least, her illnesses, imagined or otherwise, were forgotten.

She came into the bedroom and chatted brightly with Kathleen's mother while the girls did last-minute things to their hair and lipstick.

"Everyone will be so sorry you couldn't make it," Kathleen heard Mrs. Chessman declare.

"We've all been hoping that you'd crawl out of your shell and start circulating again."

"It takes time, I guess," Kathleen's mother admitted. "A shell is so nice and protected."

"Well, of course, it's a perfectly natural feeling. And you'll feel awkward at first—but only at first, I promise you."

"You do?"

Mrs. Chessman nodded solemnly. "Well, it's true that some people still have the most outlandish ideas about mental illness, but more and more people are being educated every day. It's like Mr. Chessman was saying just the other night, 'Everybody is a little bit nuts in his own way,' he said. And he's absolutely right! No one is completely normal all the time. Why, I know women who are completely wacky on the subject of *diets*. And look at me—I get every new illness that comes along, and if that doesn't make me some kind of kook, as my husband would say—"

Kathleen hurried to break up the monologue before Mrs. Chessman could expand on the subject, but she noticed that her mother didn't seem the least bit upset by the other woman's frankness. She sounded completely sincere when she asked Mrs. Chessman to drop in for coffee some morning.

Alma was quiet as she got into the back seat of the car beside Mrs. Chessman, leaving the front seat for the two girls. It wasn't the first time that Kathleen had noticed how withdrawn Alma was whenever anyone else was around. It was only when they were alone that Alma was her old self—interested, talkative, and amusing.

"It isn't just that there's a stranger in the house," she thought unhappily, looking from her father's preoccupied profile to Alma's still face, clearly caught in the rear-view mirror. It was all of them, except for Wimpy—they were a house of strangers.

Still, she had a good time at the Mother-Daughter Breakfast. When one of the women in charge expressed regret that her mother was unable to attend, it was surprisingly easy to explain that her mother wasn't feeling quite herself, but that next year she'd probably be involved in all the school affairs.

"But she *is* much better, isn't she?" the woman prodded. "I mean—I've just seen her at church, but she seems so serene and well-adjusted."

Kathleen carried home the table favor that had been at her mother's place and the good wishes of the committee members, who hoped she would be feeling well enough to join in community projects very soon.

"It wasn't a very good breakfast," she confided, sitting on the edge of her mother's bed, after she had delivered the messsage and the table favor. "Not nearly as good as Alma's breakfasts, but the hats were simply adorable. I told Mrs. Butler about the one you made, with the little chicks running around, and she said I should have brought it for the judging anyway, even though you weren't able to be there." She looked around the room. "Where is the hat, by the way? I want to show it to Marge and her mother."

"I took it apart and threw it away," her mother said. "I decided that it wasn't very amusing after all."

Kathleen said nothing, but she remembered, as if it were a face flashed suddenly on a screen, how sunny and alive her mother had looked as she worked on the silly hat. She remembered, too, the way she had hurried the two girls up- stairs and then out the front door because she was vaguely ashamed of her mother.

Later that morning her mother seemed to have forgotten the headache that had kept her home from the Mother-Daughter Break- fast. She came out into the kitchen and made a cake and a molded salad for dinner. When Wimpy ran in for his lunch and suggested that she come down to the playfield where his team was engaged in a play-off, she seemed really interested. She asked him a lot of questions about what position he played and what sort of batting average he had and how often the team had a real coach.

When Wimpy dashed off again, she went to her room, and presently she came back wearing a crisp, starched blouse and a straight skirt, A sweater was draped across her shoulders.

"I think I'll watch the game," she announced to Kathleen and Alma. "I'm sure I can find the playfield."

Kathleen looked at her doubtfully. "Do you suppose you should, Mother? I mean, it's just a midget ball club, and the field is all hot and dusty and there isn't any shade."

Her mother nodded with unaccustomed firmness. "I'd like to go."

"Then I'll go with you," Kathleen said in a resigned tone. "Dad would have a fit if we let you go wandering off by—"

"Kathleen," her mother interrupted softly, "I am not on parole, and there is absolutely no reason why I should have a chaperon every waking moment. I'd prefer going by myself."

Kathleen stared at her. "Well, of course, if you don't *want* my company," she began stiffly, but her mother didn't seem to hear. She went out the kitchen door and down the walk and turned the corner toward the playfield.

Kathleen turned and looked at Alma almost accusingly. "Now what?" she asked. "Father will be home in less than an hour and he'll want to know why we didn't stop her."

"Stop her from what?" Alma asked reasonably. "From starting to live a normal, uncomplicated life? From trying to establish a friendly relationship with her son? From being a mother?" Alma, whose voice now held a note of suppressed anger, wasn't looking at her. She polished hard at a nonexistent spot on the front of the refrigerator, and then stopped and shrugged. "Not that I'm blaming you, Kathleen—we all do it."

"We all do *what?*" Kathleen demanded. "My goodness, you sound as if we're all in some sort of conspiracy against Mother."

"Well, aren't we?" Alma sounded weary. "We've all been treating her as if she were a patient, someone to be looked after and guarded and protected—and kept hidden away."

"If you mean the Mother-Daughter Breakfast," Kathleen said defensively, "I asked her to go. I even ordered a ticket for her."

"But you didn't really want her to go."

Kathleen wanted to protest. It made her a little angry that she couldn't. "I don't know what's got into you, Alma," she said instead. "As if everything weren't upset and mixed up enough, now you have to turn against me."

Alma's voice softened. "Kathleen, you know that isn't so." All of a sudden she was very busy getting the chops out of the refrigerator, and her hands were not completely steady.

Kathleen watched her unhappily. Her mother's presence was as hard on Alma as it was on the rest of them.

She heard her father's car turn into the drive, and instead of hurrying out to meet him she went up to her room. She didn't want to see her father. He, too, had become a stranger.

8

THERE were times during the next weeks when Kathleen was almost able to forget the tension at home. She had been assigned the job of managing props for the school play. This took up a lot of her time, and her social life, thanks to Marge, Bruce, and the ever-present Swede, became more active than ever before.

Rehearsals were held after school, and sometimes after dinner as well. On these nights it became an accepted thing for Kathleen and Marge to find Bruce and Swede waiting outside the auditorium to drive them home. Several times when rehearsals were called off at the last moment, the boys seemed to know about it beforehand, and were waiting in the usual place with a plan to take them for a drive, or to the beach, or to someone's house to listen to records.

"What'll we do when the play's finished?" Margie mourned aloud on one such occasion, when they were all grouped around a beach fire. "It's been such a lovely alibi."

"You mean you need an alibi for going out with a sterling character like me?" Bruce teased her. "Don't your parents know that all the girls in town are standing in line?"

"That's what I like about you," Margie purred, "you're so modest."

Everyone laughed—everyone but Swede, who looked at Kathleen with worry in his blue eyes. "No kidding," he said, "would your folks really kick up a rumpus if they knew you were here?"

"I don't know," Kathleen admitted. "And at this point I don't care about finding out. We went to a rehearsal and the rehearsal was called off, so we went for a drive. If they ask me, I'll tell them."

Swede didn't look completely satisfied. "How come they haven't asked before this?"

She shrugged. "How should I know? Maybe they have more important things on their minds than little old me."

She said the words lightly enough, but she told herself, a trifle grimly, that this version was probably only too accurate. Normally Alma would have been checking up on her, but with Kathleen's mother at home Alma's position in the house had shifted. Everything had changed. Her father, on those rare occasions when he spent any prolonged period of time with his family, was preoccupied. Alma was always finding excuses to go out, and her mother was like a quiet, well-mannered guest. Wimpy, who lived in a world of his own, was the only one who had succeeded in making contact with her. He accepted her as naturally as though she had always been there. They held long, involved conversations about subjects like baseball and track—conversations which made Kathleen feel left out and a little resentful.

Not that she wanted her mother following her around making motherlike noises, Kathleen assured herself, but it certainly wasn't *her* fault that no one seemed the least bit interested in her comings and goings. Still— and the feeling of guilt persisted—no matter how much she assured herself that she wasn't doing anything wrong, she knew that she wasn't being completely honest, either.

"You're getting skinny again," Alma mentioned one afternoon, when Kathleen hurried home with just time to grab a sandwich and start back to school. "I'm going to have a talk with Sister Mary Catherine about the hours you've been keeping. I was awake when you came home last night and it was almost midnight."

If there was a question behind the scolding words, Kathleen pretended not to hear it.

Of course, she could have cleared up the matter once and for all by simply declining to go with the rest of them. She could say that she had orders to report home, or that she was tired, or had schoolwork to catch up on. She could even say that she didn't want to go. But then how would Swede feel?

She knew that in the "gang," the small select circle of which she had so amazingly become a part, she was being tagged as Swede's girl. There was nothing she could do about that, for a number of reasons. Swede was awkward and blundering and as trusting as a St. Bernard puppy, but Kathleen knew that he could easily be hurt, and she didn't want to be the one to do it. He was such a likable boy, not charming and magnetic like—well, like some other boys—but you always knew where you stood with a fellow like Swede. One night she had asked him about his name, whether it bothered him being nicknamed Swede.

"No, it doesn't bother me," Swede said. "Did you ever see a Texan who objected to being called Tex?"

Marge was another of the reasons she didn't want to break away from the gang. She and

Margie had been best friends for years, although they were growing a little apart these past months.

Only reluctantly would Kathleen admit to herself that the real reason she couldn't break away was Bruce.

At the beach, or driving in one of the cars, or even sitting around in someone's home listening to records, she would look up and find his dark eyes watching her with a curious brooding expression that made her heart lurch. She knew, without quite knowing how, that some day he would smile at her in a certain way and hold out his hand—and that would be it. She hoped that Margie wasn't really serious about Bruce, because it would be hard on Margie. . . .

She dashed home from school one afternoon after a brief run-through of the play to find her mother busy in the kitchen and Alma nowhere in evidence.

"Where's Alma?" she said, and pretended not to notice the odd glance her mother gave her before she answered.

"Alma's upstairs. In bed, I think."

"In *bed?* In the middle of the day? You must be kidding."

"She wasn't feeling very well," her mother said carefully. "She had a headache and a pain in her back."

117

"But Alma's never sick." Kathleen dismissed such nonsense with a shrug of her shoulders.

Her mother continued to pound flour and seasoning into the steak she had on the board. "Nevertheless, she is upstairs resting. I was just about to make some fruit juice for her. Perhaps you'd like to do that."

Kathleen made up the pitcher of juice efficiently, but her eyes were drawn again and again to the slight figure across the kitchen. It seemed to her that her mother had been losing weight steadily since she had come home. Her eyes were shadowed, too, as if she might not be sleeping very well, and she was quiet in a way that Kathleen found oddly disturbing. Kathleen knew that she had been taking her medicine faithfully; several times it was Kathy who had taken the prescription to be refilled. But her mother no longer took the pink pills that were supposed to help her sleep, and more than once Kathleen had wakened at night to hear someone pacing the floor downstairs.

She probably isn't very happy, Kathleen told herself. Maybe she wishes she'd stayed on at the hospital where everyone was so pleased with her.

She looked up to meet her mother's grave eyes and then glanced away again. "I'll take the juice up to Alma," she said abruptly.

She nudged open the door to Alma's room

with her shoulder and came in with the pitcher and glass. "Now, what is all this nonsense?" she asked lightly.

Alma, who was lying under the blanket, gave her a gentle smile. "I had a headache and a backache," she said, "so Helen shooed me off to bed. She said she could manage."

Kathleen put the pitcher on the bed stand, and then put her cool palm against Alma's forehead. "You don't look sick," she said accusingly, "and you don't seem to be running a temperature."

Alma closed her eyes. "I'm just under the weather."

Kathleen took her hand away, but she didn't move from the bedside.

"Maybe you should go down and see if you can help in the kitchen," Alma suggested at last. "But first of all I wish you'd check on Chipper. I thought I heard him down the street a little while ago, and you know that your mother can't do anything with him. She's scared to death of dogs, and he seems to know it."

"I'll check on it," Kathleen said, and then added, "I didn't realize that Mother was still scared of Chipper. I thought that was just when he was a puppy and jumped on people."

Alma opened her eyes. "There are probably

a lot of things you don't know about your mother," she said.

Kathleen went down the stairs and out the front door. She whistled to Chipper, who was far down the block, and he came bounding back. She caught him by the collar and tugged him around to the back of the house. When she had him latched in the yard, she ran up to the back door and was surprised to find it locked. Inside she could hear her mother talking softly. At first Kathleen thought she was talking to herself, but when her mother came to open the door in answer to her knock, she was so careful to close it again immediately that Kathleen looked at her in surprise.

"She isn't a bit timid now," her mother said proudly. "Sometimes she sits on my shoulder."

Miss Skylark, Kathleen's blue parakeet, was perched on the window ledge, twittering happily.

Kathleen stiffened. "I don't like her flying around the house," she said. "How did she get out of her cage?"

"I let her out."

"I'd rather she was left in her cage." Kathleen hated the note in her voice, but there didn't seem to be much she could do about it. "Pretty bird, nice bird," she said, holding out her finger and advancing on Miss Skylark cautiously. "On the finger, pretty bird, on the finger." The bird hopped on her finger and then off again, but Kathleen persisted until finally Miss Skylark was in her cage by the window. "We don't let her out except for her bath," she explained to her mother, who stood watching silently. "I lost two birds that way. Wimpy came bolting through the door and zoom—they were gone."

"I'm very careful about the doors and windows," her mother said.

"Well, just the same, I'd much prefer that Miss Skylark stayed in her cage where she belongs," Kathleen said in a tone calculated to close the matter. "Is there anything I can do to help with dinner?"

"You may set the table if you like," her mother said.

Kathleen started setting the table, banging the plates down hard. With Alma sick, she would not be able to go to a play rehearsal tonight if one were called. She would hate to miss it, for she was finding them a lot of fun. Sometimes, instead of holding a rehearsal at school, they just drove around and went over the parts informally. It wasn't as if there were anything wrong with what they were doing, Kathleen told herself piously as she put on the paper napkins, the salt and pepper, and the cream and sugar. And it certainly wasn't *her* fault that home was no longer a pleasant and friendly place.

Wimpy came galloping up onto the back porch and into the kitchen, tracking loose dirt after him.

"Wimpy Frazier, for heaven's sake, look at your shoes!" Kathleen exploded. "Don't you even know what a doormat's for?"

"Sure I know what a doormat's for—and it isn't for shoes with cleats on the bottom," her brother told her righteously. "Maybe you'd like me to leave my shoes outside, like I was living in Japan."

"I have an even better idea," Kathleen told him sweetly. "Why don't you *move* to Japan. I'll help you pack."

"Ha, ha," he said without amusement. He turned his back on her and addressed the next remark to his mother. "We beat them, ten to eight. Pretty good, huh?"

"Very good," she told him. "I hated to miss the game."

"Well, you couldn't help it," he comforted her. Then he added as an afterthought, "How's Alma?"

"Why don't you go by her door and see? Maybe you can get her an aspirin or a glass of water or something."

"O.K.," he said agreeably, and went whistling out of the kitchen and up the stairs. He brought back the information that Alma was not coming down to dinner, and that she did not want a tray, either.

Marge called just as the family was ready to sit down to eat. Her father glanced up disapprovingly when Kathleen went to the telephone. He didn't like it when her friends called and interrupted the dinner hour. He was inclined to be stuffy about things like that.

"I won't be able to rehearse tonight," Kathleen said, without even bothering to keep her voice low. "Someone else will have to cue you. Alma's sick, and things are all at sixes and sevens around here."

"I don't see how you can make Alma feel any better by staying at home," Marge argued. "Talk to your mother about it, and call me back later if she says it's O.K." She hung up while Kathleen was still protesting.

She came back to the table, aware that she was the focus of three pairs of eyes.

"Now what was all that about?" her father asked with deceptive mildness. "Is there really a rehearsal tonight?"

Kathleen looked at him warily.

"I'm not talking about a regular rehearsal," he went on. "Doesn't it occur to you that you kids are running this play business into the ground?"

Kathleen looked innocent. "I don't call the

rehearsals. And, anyway, I only went out for the play because you and Alma are always after me to join more group activities."

"I didn't mean the sort of group activities that wind up around a beach fire out at the Point—or in some hot-rod car down on the river road," her father said. "I've been doing a little checking here and there with some of the other parents, as well as with the school." He looked across the table at his daughter. "If you want to entertain your friends, you have a home, Kathleen."

Kathleen felt her cheeks burn. She glanced mutinously at her father and then at her mother. She had a home, all right—if you could call it a home. A battlefield would be more like it.

"I said I wasn't going tonight."

"That's fine," her father said unfeelingly. "And after this when there are play rehearsals, I'll be glad to drive you to school and pick you up afterward. Is that clear?"

"I'm not exactly a baby," Kathleen said. "I'm doing my schoolwork and getting passing grades."

"You are also spending a great deal of time —unauthorized time—driving around in that pink station wagon. I find it a little difficult to understand how these boys are involved in a play given by an all-girl school."

124

"They just . . . they just sort of chauffeur us around," Kathleen said lamely. "No one ever said I wasn't supposed to go. No one seemed to care much one way or another."

Her father looked at her coldly. "Now that's a stupid remark. You never even asked for permission, did you?"

Kathleen started to say something, then closed her lips firmly and looked down at her plate. She was aware that her mother was sitting there quietly, her hands in her lap. Only Wimpy was making any pretense at eating.

"We won't discuss the subject any further," Kathleen's father went on calmly. "I haven't said anything, because I was trusting your good judgment and common sense, and your honesty, but since you seem to be lacking in all these departments—"

"That isn't fair," Kathleen's mother said quietly, and both of them turned and looked at her.

Her father's brows drew together in a way that Kathleen recognized, and his voice was dangerously soft. "What isn't fair?" He was regarding his wife as if she were someone he was trying to remember.

"It isn't fair for you to blame Kathleen for something that isn't her fault. All these years you've avoided the responsibility of making decisions about the children—you've sent them to Alma. And now, with Alma no longer in charge, you expect them to bring their problems to you."

"I find it amazing," her husband said, "that you should mention my shirking my responsibilities." His tone could have cut glass. "What do you know of our family life?"

"I know more than you think," his wife said. "I know that it's because I'm back—because I'm home again that a lot of these tensions exist."

"And so?" He didn't even try to deny it.

"And so, perhaps it was a mistake, my coming home. I thought I was ready for it. I was willing to try very hard to understand my . . . my family, and what was best for them. I was willing to earn the right to have my children turn to me." She looked at Kathleen, as if for help, and not finding it there, she looked at Wimpy, who was frowning unhappily. "It's hard for everyone, the adjustment; perhaps it was too much to expect. . . ."

Kathleen got to her feet hastily, pushing back her chair. "I think I heard Alma call," she said in a strangled voice, and fled from the room without even a backward glance. Clattering up the stairs, she was aware of the ominous silence behind her.

Alma was awake and her door was open, so

Kathleen knew she must have heard some of the discussion at the dinner table.

"What's wrong, honey?" she asked at once, and as the tears welled into Kathleen's eyes, she held out her hands in the old gesture of love and compassion. "Come here and tell me all about it."

It would have been so easy to put her face down against Alma's comfortable shoulder and recite her woes into Alma's always sympathetic ear, but for some reason, unknown even to herself, Kathleen held back. She knew, vaguely, that it had something to do with the way her mother had said, "I was willing to earn the right to have my children turn to me," as if that possibility were far away and hardly worth struggling for.

It was crazy, of course; Alma had always been there and her mother had not when Kathleen needed help, but now it would be somehow disloyal to ask Alma to solve the problems that her mother's homecoming had raised.

"What's the matter, honey?" Alma asked again, and Kathleen realized that she had been standing there, staring at nothing. She straightened her shoulders and spoke quietly.

"Nothing's wrong—at least nothing that can't be straightened out. Someone told Dad about seeing Margie and me driving around in Swede's car when we were supposed to be rehearsing, so he's been pulling a heavy father act."

Alma didn't look shocked, just sorry. Sometimes Kathleen had the feeling that nothing could shock Alma. Suddenly she remembered a time, ages ago, when Wimpy had brought home some articles he had "found" in a packing box beside a hardware store. Kathleen had been horrified and so had her father, but Alma had been surprisingly calm about the whole affair. Wimpy had to take the things back, of course, but Alma refused to act as if the world had caved in because he had been guilty of this amateur pilfering. She had a matter-of-fact attitude about such childish transgressions. Alma would have been a very understanding parent.

Now she looked at Kathleen calmly and waited to hear if she were going to elaborate on her statement. That was another nice thing about Alma—she didn't ask a lot of questions.

Kathleen picked up the juice pitcher and went to the door. "Are you sure I can't bring you something to eat, Alma? It's a long time till breakfast."

But Alma shook her head firmly. "Nothing, darling. Thanks, anyway."

Kathleen went back down the stairs a few moments later. She found that Wimpy had already disappeared and that the door to her mother's room was closed. Her father was in the kitchen awkwardly piling dishes into the dishwasher.

"I'll do that," Kathleen said from the doorway.

Her father didn't answer, but he moved aside and let her take over. He didn't go back to the living room immediately, though; instead, he stood there watching her, not saying anything, but puffing thoughtfully on his pipe.

"I suppose he expects me to say that I'm sorry," Kathleen thought. "Only I'm not sorry. It's just as Mother said. He hasn't ever made it his business to check up on us. He always told me to ask Alma, and now things are so mixed up that I can't go to Alma either. And Mother wouldn't understand."

When the doorbell rang, she didn't turn from her task. Her father went out into the hallway and she heard him open the door. Swede's voice carried quite clearly to where she was standing.

"Mr. Frazier . . . um . . . I'm a sort of friend of Kathleen's. My name is Donald Henson. The . . . um . . . the kids all call me Swede."

Kathleen waited, holding her breath, and then she heard the door swing all the way open and her father say, "Kathleen is just finishing up the dishes. Come on in. I'll tell her you're here."

After her father called her, she finished wiping off the range and the front of the refrigerator. She could imagine Swede sitting uncomfortably on the edge of one of the chairs, but she didn't care. What was he doing here, anyway? No one had invited him.

Donald. She said his name under her breath as she rubbed hand lotion between her palms. No wonder he wanted people to call him Swede. He definitely wasn't the Donald type.

"Well, hi," she said, without enthusiasm, when she went into the living room. Then she added, with studied politeness, "Have you met my father?"

"I introduced myself," Swede said, getting awkwardly to his feet. "Margie said you had to stay home tonight, so I thought maybe I could just sit on the porch and talk to you or something. Unless you'd rather not, I mean."

Kathleen shrugged. "I guess it will be all right." She looked at her father. "Unless *you'd* rather we didn't," she said pointedly.

Her father regarded her unsmilingly. "You certainly don't have to sit on the porch," he said. "You can sit in here and watch television or play records. I should be doing some paper work anyway."

"I think we'd like to sit on the porch," Kathleen said. "Maybe Marge will come over when she's through with the rehearsal."

Swede said good night to her father, and then they went out to sit side by side on the wide porch steps. Swede looked at her carefully averted profile and spoke in an agonized whisper. "I'm sorry if you didn't want me to come, Kathleen. I'll get lost if you say so."

She looked at him blankly. "It's O.K. I don't mind your coming over. I'm just wondering why you did."

He grinned. "That ought to be pretty easy to figure out. I wanted to see you, and Marge said somebody was sick and you couldn't leave the house. I thought most likely your parents were just mad at you, and probably because of me—you know, on account of the beach parties and stuff. But I figured if I came over and your dad got a good look at me, he could see that I wasn't much of a menace."

It was probably the longest speech Swede had made in his life. He was a little red in the face as he paused for breath.

Kathleen stared at him. "You mean you figured it out all by yourself? That I was a damsel in distress?"

He flushed. "Hey, I didn't say that. I wanted to come over a long time ago."

"Then why didn't you?"

"Because you never asked me, I guess." He

131

chewed his lip unhappily for a few seconds. "You never ask the kids to come over—and some of them think it's on account of your mother being the way she is." He floundered for a moment and then went on. "Not that I think she's any different from anybody else, but she was away for such a long time, and she's bound to feel funny about a bunch of strange kids trooping through the house. And Marge says that your father is kind of stuffy about you getting home before ten and not dating and things like that." He was talking so fast and so earnestly that the words tripped over one another. "But he was real nice to me, your father was—invited me to come in and sit down and everything—"

"Did you expect him to pick you up and throw you off the porch?"

Swede leaned forward and peered into her face anxiously. "You aren't mad, are you?"

Kathleen didn't even try to hide her annoyance. "Why should I be mad, for goodness' sake?" She smoothed her skirt down carefully over her knees. "You came to find out if my father was really an ogre and my mother really a madwoman who goes around banging her head against the walls. It just didn't occur to you that I didn't invite you because I didn't want you around."

Swede looked as if he had been slapped, and

for a moment she felt a fierce joy at being able to hurt him. What right did he have to come around poking and prying and stumbling into things that were no concern of his?

"I'm sorry," he said. "I guess I'd better leave now." She offered no objections, and he got to his feet with awkward dignity and walked away.

Kathleen didn't move until he had turned the corner and was out of sight. Then she got up and went into the house. There was no reason why she should feel ashamed, or why her throat should be tight with tears. She didn't even *like* Swede. She didn't care if she never saw him again.

9

Marge knew all about it when she walked to school with Kathleen the next day. "I hear you had a big fight with Swede last night," she began, almost before she was out the door. "Bruce said he came home looking as if he'd just lost his last friend."

"We didn't have a fight," Kathleen said. "I just don't care to have him poking his long nose into my business, that's all."

Marge looked offended. "But I thought you liked Swede."

"I don't like him *that* much," Kathleen said distinctly.

"It was probably my fault that he dropped in like that without an invitation," Marge said.

"He wanted to know if it would be all right, and I said I thought it would, because you know how parents, and especially fathers, are about meeting the boys their daughter runs around with—"

"Do we *have* to talk about it?" Kathleen broke in. "I mean, is there any reason we have to chew the subject like a bone?"

Marge gave her a slow, careful look from under artfully curled lashes. "No, we don't have to talk about it," she said. "We don't have to talk at all if you'd rather not—but you don't mind my pointing out that you're getting pretty touchy all of a sudden? Everyone notices it. You snap at people for no reason at all. You seem to have a gripe against the entire world."

Kathleen said nothing. She told herself it was because such a stupid remark called for no answer, but she couldn't quite dismiss the feeling that it held more than a grain of truth. It was the sort of thing that Wimpy had been telling her. "How come you're such a crab nowadays? You never used to care if Chipper jumped on you—and now you yell at him."

She thought back and knew that she had been difficult to live with these past weeks. She could even remember the day it had started—the day she had learned that her mother was coming home again.

It wasn't that she didn't like her mother. She

135

might even learn to love her. It was just that things were so unreal, as if all of them were walking around in a curious vacuum, waiting for something to happen.

Waiting for Mother to have one of her spells, Kathleen suddenly admitted to herself. Waiting for all the fright and confusion to start over again. Waiting for her mother to go back to that place.

By the time they got to school, Kathleen was able to put her hand on Marge's arm and speak almost normally. "I'm sorry, Margie. Forgive me?"

Marge gave her a quick smile. That was one of the nice things about her, she seldom held a grudge. "Skip it," she said happily.

At school they were all issued tickets to the play, and it was announced that each girl was expected to dispose of at least six tickets. Kathleen tucked the small squares of yellow cardboard into her purse, thinking a little glumly that she'd have to ask her family to buy them. Her father, and Alma, and Wimpy, and probably her mother—even as she counted them off in her mind, she knew it was wrong that she still thought of her mother last. That meant two tickets left over. She probably could have gotten Swede to take them, if she hadn't alienated him forever by being so surly last night when he was only trying to help. Then she thought of the way Swede had looked at her last night. Chipper had looked at her in almost that same way when she had slapped him for jumping on her new skirt. Wimpy looked that way when she yelled at him for messing up his room. A sad look that could change to forgiveness the moment she smiled.

She felt a little happier as she went into her first class. A new comic book would set things straight with Wimpy, and Chipper would be happy to settle for a bone picked up at the corner market. Of course, she couldn't very well have a bone or a comic book gift-wrapped and sent to Swede.

Marge nudged her. "Now what's the matter?" she asked curiously. "A minute ago you were as glum as the inside of a black cloud, and now you're grinning as if you knew a wicked secret."

"I'll tell you later," Kathleen whispered, and went on to her own place across the room.

Marge took eighteen tickets to sell. But then, why not? She had relatives all over the place, and after all she was the star of the production.

Kathleen hurried home from school buoyed up by her new resolutions. She was going to be cheerful and helpful if it killed her. She wouldn't say a word when Wimpy tracked in dirt, or ate with his fingers, or whistled off key. She would ask her mother to go shopping with her just as soon as the play was over. Her mother was still wearing the clothes she had brought from the hospital and a few things she had ordered through catalogs.

Alma, who had apparently recovered from her sick spell, was scrubbing the kitchen when Kathleen came in. She sat back on her heels and blew a wisp of hair away from her cheek. "I'm just finished," she said. "You can apply the wax as soon as the floor dries."

"O.K.," Kathleen said, and glanced toward the hall door as she added, "where's Mother?"

"She went to watch Wimpy play baseball. She should be back any minute." Alma got up and stretched. "There's a roast in the oven, and your mother made some gingerbread for dinner. You can put the potatoes around the roast while you're waiting for the floor to dry. I'll have to be getting dressed pretty soon. Margaret is picking me up to go to the Community Theater, and we're going to dinner beforehand."

Kathleen listened, only half hearing what Alma was saying. Gingerbread. Yes, now that Alma mentioned it, she could smell it, but today she hadn't even noticed; she hadn't been apprehensive and frightened. She hadn't even *noticed!*

Alma gave her an odd look. "What's the matter, honey?"

Kathleen found a smile and the right words.

"I was just thinking that you seem to have an active social life all of a sudden," she said. "Are you trying to grow away from us, Alma?"

Alma looked startled for a moment, then she managed a faint grin. "I guess I'm not a very good actress. I didn't know I was being so obvious." She rinsed her hands off under the water tap, and then dried them on a paper towel. "I think we'll agree, though, Kathleen, that it is high time I was making a life of my own—apart from the Fraziers."

"Is that why you pretended to be sick yesterday? And why you always make excuses to go to another Mass on Sunday, and why you go straight to your room after dinner, instead of staying down and watching television with the rest of us?"

Alma flushed. "My acting is evidently worse than I realized."

"I think all of us have known what's been going on." Kathleen felt very grown-up and wise as she made this statement, but she was in no way prepared for Alma's next announcement.

"Kathleen," she asked gravely, "what would you say if I told you I was thinking about getting married?"

Kathleen swallowed. "You . . . you aren't kidding me, are you?"

Alma smiled. "No, honey, I'm not kidding

you. At my age, it isn't a kidding matter."

"But—but *Alma.*" She hesitated and then plunged on doggedly. "You haven't ever seemed to be interested in anyone. I mean . . . well, you don't just decide to get married and then walk down the street and find someone."

"No, not like that," Alma admitted. "But this really isn't any spur-of-the-moment thing. I've known Henry for several years."

"Henry?" Kathleen's eyebrows shot up. "Henry Graham? The insurance man?"

Alma nodded. "Yes, Henry Graham."

"But . . . but he's got that big family," Kathleen spluttered. "And everyone says those Graham kids are little monsters—they've simply been running wild since their mother died."

"Exactly," Alma said, as if this were an argument in favor of the marriage. "They need someone—and I need someone."

Kathleen bit her lip. "But Alma, this is something you can't go rushing into. You have to think about it."

"I've been thinking about it," Alma said. "Henry and I aren't going to elope, you know. We're both adult, sensible people. He needs a housekeeper and a mother for his children. We would both have to make allowances and adjustments."

"It doesn't sound like much of a marriage," Kathleen said bleakly. "It would be bad enough losing you, Alma, but I'd hate to think of you tied up with a family like that. Wouldn't you feel that . . . that they were just using you?"

"I'd feel that I was needed, Kit. That's pretty important to a woman." Alma got the can of wax from the cupboard and put it on the drainboard. "There is much to be said for companionship, too. It's hard for young people to realize; youth is so often concerned with the romantic side of marriage. But Henry and I have a lot in common. We attend the same church, know the same people, feel the same way about important things—and I think Henry's children like me." She nodded her head. "Yes, it could work out very well."

"But it sounds so cold-blooded," Kathleen couldn't help saying. "Marriage has to be something more than just a job that needs doing." And then she added, uncertainly, "Doesn't it?"

The conversation with Alma left Kathleen upset. When Alma had gone upstairs to get ready for her dinner engagement, Kathleen peeled potatoes to put around the roast. Then she waxed the kitchen floor and read a movie magazine while she waited for the wax to dry.

It might have been twenty minutes later, it could have been an hour, when she heard the dread sound of brakes applied too suddenly—and then the crumbling of metal and splintering of glass. Over it all came a thin, piercing scream.

She didn't know how she knew it was her mother's voice. She just knew, and in seconds she was across the kitchen and down the steps and into the street, where a white-faced man was climbing from a car which had come to an abrupt stop against a telephone pole.

"I didn't even see her," he was saying. "She shot out into the street like a bullet, and I jerked the wheel and plowed into the telephone pole—I couldn't avoid hitting the dog. . . ."

Kathleen heard him with only half her mind. All she could see was her mother, sitting on the curb, with Chipper gathered up into her arms.

A crowd gathered almost at once. A man was leaning over Kathleen's mother, talking to her and trying to take the dog. But she was holding fiercely to the large, shaggy animal, seemingly unmindful of the fact that his blood was staining her skirt and blouse, and that tears were streaming down her face.

"It's my fault," she whispered, as Kathleen knelt beside her. "I told Wimpy that I'd bring his dog home and put him in the yard. But he saw the cat across the street and ran away from me. . . ."

"It wasn't your fault," Kathleen said in a

choked voice. "It could happen to anyone. Wimpy shouldn't have asked you to bring Chipper home. He knew you were afraid of him."

"No, he didn't, I never let him know. I didn't want him to think I was a sissy." She went on stroking the dog's head as she talked. "But Chipper knew I was afraid." She looked down at the dog. "You knew I was afraid, didn't you, boy? You knew."

"I'm afraid he's dead," Kathleen said faintly.

Her mother looked at her fearfully. "He couldn't be dead. He's Wimpy's dog. He trusted me to take care of him. . . ."

The crowd was starting to break up. People drifted away, looking back to see if there was going to be any more excitement. A small figure was running down the block. Kathleen knew that it was Wimpy, even before she saw him stop, and then walk slowly toward them.

"I couldn't avoid hitting the dog," the man was still saying. "Should have been on a leash anyway. . . ."

Kathleen got up slowly and faced her brother. She wanted to turn and run away so that she didn't have to look at him, but she stood her ground and tried to think of something to say. "It wasn't Mother's fault," she heard herself saying. "She was trying to put him in the yard, and he saw Colby's cat and pulled away from her."

Wimpy knelt down beside his mother and touched her arm. "Let me have him," he said. "He's bleeding all over you."

She looked at him with eyes that shared his grief. "Wimpy, I'm so sorry."

"He was just a dog," Wimpy said brokenly.

He picked up the dog and no one offered to help, even though Chipper was almost as big as the boy. Half-carrying and half-dragging him, he got his pet across the sidewalk and through the gate that Kathleen ran to hold open. Alma had come out on the porch, but she said nothing. What was there to say to a boy who had just lost his dearest friend and companion?

Kathleen went back and put her arms around her mother's shoulders. "Come on, Mother, let's go inside."

But her mother continued to sit there, crying softly but uncontrollably into her two blood-smeared palms. A car came around the corner and pulled to a jarring stop. Kathleen's father jumped out.

"It must be later than I realized," Kathleen thought. "It must be after five thirty—Father never gets home before five thirty. I wonder if the potatoes are cooked?"

"What happened?" he asked, and Kathleen

told him as quietly as she could. She hadn't known that she was crying until she found the words choking in her throat.

"I see." He leaned over then and picked up his wife as easily as if she had been a child, and carried her into the house. "Don't cry, darling," Kathleen heard him whisper to her. "Please don't cry, darling." He carried her in and put her on the davenport, and Alma came running with a quilt and a cold cloth to wash the tears away.

"Let her cry," Alma said softly, and shooed Kathleen ahead of her into the kitchen, closing the door behind them. "Now," she said briskly, "wash your face and try to pull yourself together. This is going to be hard enough for Wimpy without having the rest of us fall apart." There were tears in Alma's eyes, too, but she went out on the back porch and down the path to where Wimpy was sitting quietly on the ground beside his dog.

Kathleen washed her face and pulled a comb through her hair, and when Alma came back into the house, she went out to Wimpy. He was gently stroking Chipper's rough coat and staring off into the distance.

"It wasn't Mother's fault," he said. "I shouldn't have asked her to bring him home. She's afraid of dogs, especially big dogs like Chipper."

Kathleen nodded wordlessly.

"She was getting better, though," Wimpy went on.

"She hardly jumped at all when Chipper licked her hand. Lots of times she used to take his water pan and put cold water in it. I think she might have liked Chipper after a while."

"I'm sure she would," Kathleen said, knowing that was what he would want to hear. Then, when the silence had become almost intolerable, she whispered, "Wimpy, do you think I should call the man from the Humane Society to come and take him away?"

He looked at her uncomprehendingly at first, and then shook his head. "Not yet," he said. "I think I'll just let him sleep here tonight. He used to like to sleep out here."

Kathleen turned abruptly and went back into the house.

It seemed hours later when her father came in from the living room and told her that her mother was asleep. "Where's Wimpy?" he asked, and she nodded in the direction of the door.

"He's still sitting out there. I didn't think I should tell him to come in and eat. I . . . I don't imagine he feels much like food at this point."

"That's right. He'll come in when he's ready."

"You haven't eaten either," Kathleen reminded him.

Her father sat down to dinner then, but he didn't eat much, and after the dishes were cleared away, there didn't seem to be anything to talk about.

Alma had gone with Margaret to the theater. It seemed strange that she should walk away from them in their troubled hour, but maybe she thought it would be for the best. Trouble and worry were supposed to pull families together, and Alma was trying to break the ties that held them to her.

Kathleen tiptoed to the door and looked in at her mother, who was still sleeping soundly, although there were tear streaks along her cheeks. She looked young and very vulnerable lying there, like a tired child.

"Still asleep?" Kathleen's father asked, and she nodded.

"Yes, still asleep."

She left slices of the roast beef on a plate in the refrigerator before she got ready for bed. And she cut a generous slab of the gingerbread and left it on the edge of the table where Wimpy would be sure to see it when he came in.

When she went upstairs to bed, her father was sitting in the big chair by the davenport —not reading or watching television, but just sitting there with his head back and his eyes closed. Wimpy was still keeping his lonely vigil beside his dog.

She slept fitfully. Several times she wakened, thinking that she heard voices downstairs, or that she heard Wimpy's slow footsteps dragging up the stairs.

Her dreams were troubled. Dark, shadowy figures spun in and out, none of them quite solid enough for Kathleen to identify, and she wakened with the dull feeling that she had been walking for miles and miles along a road that led nowhere.

10

KATHLEEN KNEW, of course, that her mother wrote to Dr. Lundigan and his wife. She even knew that they answered the letters, but she was in no way prepared when the doctor dropped into town for a visit.

He was there when she came in from school, sitting at the kitchen table with her mother and Alma, having a cup of coffee. It was all very casual. He explained that he was driving through town and thought he'd stop and look in on them. And he indicated that it would take very little urging to persuade him to stay for dinner.

Kathleen couldn't have explained how she knew, even in that first moment, that Dr. Lundigan was worried and displeased. The conviction grew as the afternoon wore on. It had something to do with the way he 'looked at her mother, and the probing questions he asked.

"How is your tennis game coming along?" he asked once, and looked unhappy when Kathleen's mother simply smiled and shook her head. "You mean you haven't started? But that was one of the things you were looking forward to, wasn't it?"

A little later he asked, "Do you play the piano any more?" When she shrugged off the question, his mouth tightened again.

Shortly before dinner Alma asked Kathleen to go down to the supermarket for her, and Dr. Lundigan went with her. "I need the exercise, and I'd like to get a look at the town," he explained easily, but Kathleen knew that it was just an excuse to get her off by herself.

Still, there was no graceful way that she could refuse his company. He strode along beside her in heavy silence until they were out of sight of the house, and then he turned and looked at her searchingly. "It isn't working out, is it?" he said. "What happened?"

"You mean about Mother?" she asked carefully.

"Naturally, I mean about your mother. She looks terrible. She hasn't been sleeping, she's thin, and she doesn't get out enough." He puffed on his pipe for a moment, and then went on. "I shouldn't have let her come home. She'd have had a better chance with strangers."

Kathleen stared at him. "What do you mean, with strangers?"

"It happens more often than you'd think," Dr. Lundigan told her. "Especially in a case like this where there has been a long separation. The adjustment is too difficult for everyone."

"I thought we were getting along very well," Kathleen said.

The doctor looked at her gravely. "Did you? Did you really think that, Kathleen?"

He didn't say it accusingly, and there was absolutely no reason she should feel uneasy—except that she remembered her mother saying, "I was willing to try very hard to understand my family. I thought I was ready for it."

Kathleen spoke quickly to cover her feeling of guilt. "It's bound to take a little time—you said that yourself."

"She's been home for almost six weeks, time enough to give us an indication of whether the experiment will be a success or a failure." He said the words flatly, as if he didn't need any more evidence—as if he had already made up his mind. Kathleen experienced a little sense of panic.

"She's especially upset right now because of Wimpy's dog. Did . . . did she tell you about that?"

"She told me."

"But wouldn't that make a difference?

Wouldn't that account for some of her nervousness?"

"A well-adjusted person takes these things in stride," Dr. Lundigan pointed out. "She doesn't torture herself over a dog being hit by a car."

"It wasn't just a dog," Kathleen said. "It was Wimpy's dog." She stopped just on the verge of explaining that Wimpy was her mother's only friend—the only one who had really accepted her and made her feel necessary and wanted.

"I was so sure she'd be all right," the doctor went on, as if he were thinking aloud. "She tried so hard." He turned his head then, and took his pipe out of his mouth and spoke earnestly. "She even subscribed to one of those teen-age magazines the last year she was with us. She read all the stories and articles so that she'd be able to communicate with you a little better. That's the very word she used, *communicate*. She asked me if it were possible to take a mail-order course in motherhood, because that seemed to be the only course open to her."

Kathleen swallowed. "I was always going to go shopping with her. She never asked, so I expect she was waiting for me to make the first move."

"Why didn't you make the first move?" he asked. "It would help a lot if I knew."

"I don't know," Kathleen said unsteadily. "I expect it's because I was more interested in my own affairs."

He looked at her somberly. "But Kathleen, this *was* your own affair."

They didn't talk much after that, but she couldn't shake off the feeling that Dr. Lundigan was deeply disappointed in her.

It was the night of the final dress rehearsal at school, but Kathleen didn't want to go. She was almost afraid to leave the house, because she didn't know what Dr. Lundigan would say to her father or what he would say in return.

"You have to go," Alma told her sternly. "The entire cast would freeze up if they didn't know you were there in the wings ready to prompt them."

"I know I have to go," Kathleen said. "But it seems so much more important to stay here and make Dr. Lundigan understand . . . about Mother."

Alma looked at her. "Understand what, honey?"

"That . . . that it's our fault she isn't better. That we haven't really given her a chance, until now."

Alma nodded as if this garbled message made perfectly good sense. "Then why don't you tell the doctor yourself, before you go to the rehearsal?"

"I couldn't," Kathleen whispered.

"I think you could," Alma said. "But first of all why not go in and see if you can help your mother with a zipper or anything. She's getting dressed to go for a drive with your father and the doctor."

"Are . . . are they going to talk about Mother going back to the hospital?" Kathleen asked.

"I don't know."

Kathleen went and knocked on the bedroom door, and her mother asked her to come in.

Kathleen saw at once that her mother wasn't having trouble with zippers or anything else. For a change, she looked very relaxed and happy. She was trying to do something new with her hair, but it wasn't what could be called an unqualified success.

"I think it's long enough for a French roll," Kathleen heard herself saying. "That is, if you want me to try. . . ."

Her mother half turned on the dressing-table bench and gave her a shy smile. "Would you, Kathy? I seem to be all thumbs."

Kathleen picked up the brush and started to work. She had a special knack with hair, and as she brushed she had the oddest feeling that for the first time since her mother had come back, she was giving her something.

"I like that brown dress," Kathleen said, when their eyes met in the dressing-table mirror. "It's new, isn't it?"

"One of the mail-order dresses," her mother said. "I was quite pleasantly surprised."

"You look . . . very nice," Kathleen said. If she had been talking to Alma, she could have tossed off something like, "Alma, you look perfectly ravishing in that new dress." It was strange and somehow disturbing that with her mother, who needed the reassurance of a compliment so much more than Alma, she was awkward and tongue-tied.

It's too soon, Kathleen told herself, as she put the last few hairpins in place and stood back to admire her handiwork. Later, when we're a little more at ease with one another, I'll be able to say things like that without sounding sticky.

To her mother she only said, "Don't move a muscle till I get some hair spray. We'll anchor all the loose hairs before you start breathing again. O.K.?"

Her mother smiled. "O.K."

Kathleen ran and got the hair spray from the upstairs bedroom. Her mother closed her eyes obediently while Kathleen sprayed her new hairdo.

"There, all done," she said at last. "Do you like it?"

Her mother scarcely glanced at her hair. She was looking at Kathleen, and her eyes threatened tears. "Thank you, dear," she said gently. "Thank you very much."

It was time to get started if she was going to the dress rehearsal. Marge would be waiting. But she took the time to go into the study where her father and Dr. Lundigan were having their coffee and talking quietly together. Both men looked a little surprised when she came to the doorway and knocked timidly.

"What is it, Kathy? Want a lift to the rehearsal?"

She shook her head. "No. I just wanted to say good night to Dr. Lundigan, and to . . . to ask him something." She came in, closed the door behind her, and leaned against it. Her heart was pounding so hard that she was sure they could hear it.

Dr. Lundigan looked at her with mild surprise. "Yes?"

"I hope . . . I hope you won't decide anything about Mother until we've had another chance." She glanced at her father and then away again. "At least, until I've had another chance. I haven't been much of a daughter; but I'll really try, Dr. Lundigan, I promise you I will."

The doctor nodded. "Kathleen, I can only tell you that I shall do what I honestly think is best for your mother."

She swallowed. "I guess I can't ask for any more." She put out her hand, and the doctor took it solemnly. "Good-bye, Dr. Lundigan."

"Good-bye, Kathleen. And I hope your play is a howling success."

She glanced at her wristwatch. "Oh, I'm fifteen minutes late! Marge will be fuming."

Marge wasn't angry when Kathy ran up and knocked at the door. Marge wasn't even home. Her father had taken her to the auditorium.

Kathy tried to bite back her exasperation as she hurried along toward the school. How exactly like Margie to go off and leave her, as if Kathleen hadn't waited for her dozens of times. She was halfway there when a familiar honk signaled the approach of Swede's pink station wagon. The car drew up alongside, and Bruce grinned at her.

"Hop in," he said. "You're going to be late."

She scrambled in without any argument. "I *am* late. We ran into some confusion at home." She glanced at Swede, who was looking acutely miserable. "Hi," she said, and gave him a quick smile. "I'm really sorry about the other night. I was worried about something else and I took it out on you."

"That's O.K.," he said, turning red, but looking happy at the same time.

Bruce turned his shoulder to cut off her view of Swede. "You haven't said hello to me yet," he pointed out. "Hi, Kathleen."

"Hi," she said, and felt the familiar glow

that started at her toes whenever Bruce looked at her.

"Well, tomorrow night it will be all over," he said. "I suppose you have to go to the cast party after the show?"

She nodded. "I suppose so. Everyone's going."

"It'll break up early, though," Bruce said. "Maybe you'll go out with me afterward. I can borrow a car."

He was talking softly, but of course Swede could hear every word. Kathleen knew by the way Swede's hands were tight on the wheel that he was waiting for her reply, too. It wasn't fair that Swede should be there when Bruce asked her to go out with him. Was Bruce a complete idiot not to realize—

She looked up at Bruce, who was as good-looking and charming as ever. She looked into his warm, dark eyes and had the oddest feeling that she couldn't see her own reflection mirrored in them. All you could see was Bruce. You couldn't tell what he was thinking or feeling, you didn't have any idea what was going on behind his easy smile.

All you had to do was look at Swede to tell that he was utterly miserable or outrageously happy. Swede had that kind of face. It told all. Swede probably knew that he could never compete with a personality boy like Bruce, just as Kathleen had always known that the boys would find Marge more attractive. It gave her a feeling of kinship with him, almost as if she could look inside Swede's head and see the wheels going around.

Swede would never be relaxed and confident and superbly arrogant as Bruce was—and Kathleen would never be gay and sparkling like Marge. . . .

"What about Margie?" Kathleen heard herself ask, and knew by the way Bruce smiled that he had been waiting for this question.

"Who," Bruce asked, "is Margie?"

They had reached the auditorium and Swede pulled up with a jerk.

"Thanks," Kathleen said, and opened the door on her side, but Bruce's hand on her own stopped her before she could get out.

"You haven't answered me," he said, but not as if he were at all worried—not as if he even considered that there might be two answers.

Kathleen looked down at the brown hand covering hers, and thought how strange and unfair it was that having Bruce touch her hand had the impact of a stab of electricity. "I don't know," she said. "I really don't know, Bruce."

His fingers closed over hers. "Well, think about it, Valentine."

When the car had driven off, she could still hear the echo of Bruce's teasing voice. *Valentine*. . . .

So he had known all the time that she was the one.

She hurried into the auditorium and took her place in the wings. The first act was already in progress, and Margie was just about to make her entrance. She paused beside Kathleen for a split second.

"I couldn't wait, Kathy. I had to get dressed and everything."

"It was O.K.," Kathleen said. "I got a ride."

"I knew your father would bring you."

"Father had company and couldn't leave," Kathleen said, and then added, because she couldn't seem to help herself, "Bruce and Swede picked me up."

Margie's quickly averted glance told her all she needed to know. So Bruce and Marge *had* quarreled. Kathleen wondered why she wasn't more elated about it. It was what she had wanted, wasn't it?

Well, wasn't it?

The rehearsal dragged on for a long, long time. Kathleen had a headache before it was over. She was glad to see that her father was waiting to drive Margie and her home.

"Did Dr. Lundigan leave?" she asked immediately, and her father nodded.

"Yes, he left."

She couldn't ask any more questions—not with Margie sitting there, all ears. They dropped Margie off at her house, drove the car into the garage, and finally went into the house.

Alma was waiting in the kitchen. "Did you

take Helen with you?" she asked at once. "She isn't in her room. I went in to talk to her and she was gone."

Kathleen's father brushed past Alma into the charming, empty room. "That's impossible. Where would she go?"

"I don't know. I was worried about her. She gave me a strange look when I came out of the study this evening, after Dr. Lundigan had called me in there to talk to me."

"Well, she certainly couldn't have gone very far," Kathleen said, more positively than she was feeling. "Was she here when you left, Father?"

He nodded his head slowly, frowning. "She must have been. She excused herself and went to bed around ten o'clock, before Dr. Lundigan left. She seemed perfectly all right all evening."

"She went to bed *before* Dr. Lundigan left? You're sure?" Kathleen had visions of her mother hiding in the back of Dr. Lundigan's station wagon. She knew it was preposterous, but it was the first thing that entered her mind. It was the sort of thing that an . . . an unbalanced person might do. But her mother wasn't unbalanced. She was perfectly rational, and tonight she had seemed really happy.

"What shall we do?" Alma asked. "I suppose we ought to notify someone."

"She probably just went out for a walk," Kathleen's father said without conviction. "Or she decided to walk down and watch Kathy's play rehearsal. She was saying tonight in the car that she was hoping you'd ask her to go with you—that she thought play rehearsals were a lot more fun than the finished product."

"I never thought of it," Kathleen said. "But she wouldn't be out walking this late at night unless . . . unless she wasn't herself. . . ."

Her father gave her a troubled look. "She was more like herself, her old self, than she has seemed since she's been home."

He's afraid, too, Kathy told herself. He's afraid, as I am, that we failed, that it's too late to help her, that we didn't try hard enough.

"Do you suppose she could have gone back to the hospital with Dr. Lundigan?" Alma spoke the words aloud and both of them looked at her thankfully.

"Why would she do that?" Kathleen's father sounded cross, but Kathleen knew it was the tone he used to hide his real feelings.

"Why wouldn't she?" Alma asked reasonably. "She isn't happy. There isn't any reason why she should feel happy or welcomed, or even needed here. That's why I wanted to tell her tonight that I'm leaving, that I'm going to marry Henry Graham."

Kathleen knew by the stunned look on her father's face that he had never even considered that Alma might leave them and go on to a life of her own.

"It doesn't seem like very good timing," Alma went on, "but I thought you ought to know, too. I told Kathleen several days ago."

Kathleen dragged her voice up from somewhere deep inside her. "I didn't say anything because it was Alma's secret. When . . . when you get used to the idea you can see that it will be a very good thing. Mr. Graham is awfully nice, and the kids will settle down when Alma gets hold of them."

"I see," Kathleen's father said, as if he didn't see at all. Then he turned to his daughter and said harshly, "What are we going to do? We can't just stand here. There must be somewhere we can start looking."

As quickly as that he turned aside from Alma's problem. He hadn't even said that he hoped she'd be happy.

Wimpy came trailing down the stairs in his pajamas when he heard them talking. He looked startled, and then thoughtful, when Kathleen explained what had happened.

"Well, she wouldn't go out walking in the middle of the night unless she was *going* somewhere," he said. "What do you think she is, some kind of nut?"

There was a thudding silence, and then his father spoke gently. "No, Wimpy, we don't think she's some kind of nut, but we're worried about her. Do you have any idea where she might have gone?"

Wimpy shook his head. "No. But she must have had a reason. Did anything happen?"

"No. Nothing happened. Go back to bed, Wimpy, she'll probably be along any minute."

As if on cue, there was the sound of a car door slamming, and the unmistakable tapping of a woman's footsteps. The car roared away up the street, and Kathleen's mother came around the house and up to the back porch. She walked lightly, cradling something in the crook of her arm. And she looked only slightly astonished to find all of them standing there waiting for her.

"I'm sorry," she said. "I was hoping you wouldn't miss me. There was something I had to attend to and I wasn't sure there'd be enough time." She walked over to Wimpy, and put the blanket-wrapped, squirming bundle she held into his arms.

"She won't grow as big as Chipper, but the man says that she'll make a wonderful pet. She doesn't have a name, so you can take your time and think of a good one."

Wimpy stared at the puppy, who had squirmed free of the blanket and was sniffing and whining. He held the little thing up against his cheek, and the tears he had never been able to shed for Chipper ran down into the soft fur. "I don't want another dog," he choked. "I gave away my doghouse and the leash and everything. . . ."

The puppy licked his face and made a whimpering sound. It was such a little dog. You couldn't imagine this puppy catching a baseball or tumbling in the grass or pulling a wagon. Wimpy looked up at his mother with sorrowful eyes. "I'll make a bed in a basket and put a clock in it, the way we did for Chipper when he was a pup. Then he won't cry all night."

"It's a female," his mother said. "If you really don't want another dog, you can take her back to Mr. Perkins in a few days. He'll be glad to let you have another pet in exchange."

Wimpy held the puppy's head down against his shoulder and started scratching behind its ear, almost automatically. "You mean you walked all the way out to Mr. Perkins' place and got this puppy *tonight?*"

"No. I called a cab from the cab stand down on the next corner, and then Mr. Perkins drove me home."

"Yeah, but going there in the middle of the *night,*" Wimpy grumbled. "He must think you're some kind of a nut!"

11

KATHLEEN WAKENED early the next morning, and for a few moments she stretched and yawned without even trying to identify the blissful languor that possessed her. All the tensions and unhappiness of the past weeks somehow had been dissolved in the events of last night.

Her mother had looked so different standing there with her chin up and her eyes bright and her voice only a little unsteady. "When Dr. Lundigan came here today, I thought that it was just a friendly visit. Then I noticed the way he kept looking at me, as if he were sorry, and I was sure that one of you had sent for him."

Kathleen gasped. "But why would we do that?"

"Because the probation period is almost over, and maybe you felt I should go back." She looked at her husband as she spoke, and then at Kathy, and finally at Alma. "I couldn't blame you, because I haven't made much of an adjustment. But before the day was over, you all seemed to be helping me—the way I had thought you might when I first came back."

Alma found her voice then, and she sounded very tired. "I'm sorrier than I can say. That's what I was going to tell you tonight—that's how we discovered that you were gone."

"I had to get Wimpy's dog, because if Dr. Lundigan was thinking about taking me back, there might not be enough time. So I slipped out of the house while you were still talking in the study." She stopped then and looked at her son. "Why don't you fix the dog a bed by the furnace?" she suggested. "Just for tonight, until we decide what should be done with her."

Wimpy nodded solemnly. "O.K." He came over and rubbed his head against his mother's shoulder, a gesture of affection rare for Wimpy. "Thank you," he said.

She dropped a swift kiss on his cheek. "Bed your dog down, and then run along to bed yourself. O.K.?"

Kathleen's father folded his arms, leaned back against the table, and looked around at the three women. "Look," he said, "we've all been going at this the wrong way. I had a long

167

talk with Dr. Lundigan, and he set me straight on a lot of things. As soon as school is out and things are squared away around here, Helen is going away for a little trip." He looked at his wife and continued softly, "We're *both* going away on a little trip, a sort of delayed honeymoon." He looked at Kathy then, and she nodded quickly. "Then, when we come home again, we'll cope with one problem at a time —beginning with a wedding." He swung around and smiled at Alma, who was standing quietly by the door watching him. "You will let us give you a wedding?"

"Of course," she said.

Kathleen's father sobered then. "Only don't rush into anything, will you? Because even though there's a lot to be said for companionship and understanding and all the rest of it, if you don't have love, you don't have anything."

Kathleen's eyes smarted with tears. She looked at her mother, whose face showed that she was just beginning to understand what all this was about.

"I don't know about the rest of you," Kathleen said clearly, "but I'm so tired I'm absolutely stupid, and tomorrow promises to be another long day."

Her father put his arm around her shoulders and gave her a quick squeeze. "That's right," he said. "We have a lot of tomorrows coming up."

She went up the stairs, and after a few moments she heard Alma follow her. It was a temptation to slip into Alma's room and tell her —tell her what? Alma *knew*, without being told, how much they loved her and depended on her. She knew that she would always hold a very special place in all their hearts; she even knew how much they would miss her. Kathleen climbed wearily into bed and clicked off the bedside light.

Before she knew it, the sun was shining and it was morning. She leaped out of bed and went to the window to identify the sound that had wakened her. The new puppy was in an improvised pen in the side yard, yapping steadily. Even as Kathy watched, Wimpy came out of the kitchen carrying a bowl carefully between his two hands. The puppy leaped up and lapped happily at the milk, pausing only to lavish moist licks on Wimpy's hands.

Kathleen dressed and went downstairs to the kitchen, where her mother and Alma were having their breakfast. They were talking about the wedding, making plans, just as if it were all settled.

The telephone rang, and it was Marge, having last-minute jitters and wanting Kathy's comfort and support.

"I can't come over right this minute," Kathleen told her. "I have a lot of things to do. My room is an absolute mess, and I promised Mother I'd get it straightened up this morning."

Marge let this somewhat surprising excuse slip by unnoticed. It was perfectly evident that she had other things on her mind. "When you saw Bruce last night," she said at last, "did he say anything about the cast party?"

"Why?" Kathleen said.

"I asked him if he wanted to go," Margie said. "Mrs. David said we could invite some of our friends, so I told Bruce that if he felt like coming, and bringing Swede—"

"It's the other way around, isn't it?" Kathleen asked calmly. "I mean, Swede comes and brings Bruce."

There was a moment of surprised silence, and then Marge demanded petulantly, "What in the world's the matter with you this morning? Maybe you'd better go back to bed and get up on the right side."

"Maybe I should," Kathleen agreed. "Goodbye, Margie."

She hung up the telephone and went out in the kitchen to have breakfast. Presently Wimpy came in to join her. He had made a determined effort to wash up, but he still smelled faintly of dog, and his eyes, when he looked at Kathy, had lost their haunted look.

"Tonight the play will be finished," Kathy

announced to the room at large, "and next Friday school will be over for the summer."

They all looked at her as if they expected her to add something to this announcement, but Kathy went on eating dreamily. *The old order changeth, yielding place to new,* she thought.

She looked at her mother, who no longer seemed a stranger, and at Wimpy, tipped far back in his chair, trying to peer out the window at his puppy. She looked at Alma, who was watching her with the intentness that meant she knew pretty much what Kathleen was feeling. Later on, she told herself, I'll call and make peace with Margie. After all, it isn't her fault that I feel guilty about Bruce. . . .

When Wimpy had excused himself to go outside, Kathy continued to sit at the table listening to her mother and Alma talk about menus and people who should be put on the invitation list.

When her mother got up to go to the telephone and Alma began to clear the dishes away, Kathleen propped her elbows on the table and spoke mildly. "People are funny, aren't they? I was just thinking. . . ."

Alma waited, looking interested.

"I was just thinking about this girl at school who has this simply mad crush on a boy," Kathleen went on carefully. "I mean this isn't anything new, it's been going on for years. She gets goose pimples when she sees him walking down the street, and when he smiles at her, her knees turn to jelly." She looked up, and Alma nodded, as if she knew exactly what Kathleen meant. "So now he's finally asked her to go out with him, and she doesn't know whether she wants to go or not. Did you ever hear of anything so weird?"

"It doesn't sound weird to me," Alma said reasonably. "Maybe she has sense enough to know that a mad crush isn't anything very permanent, and she prefers a nice familiar dream to a disappointing reality."

"But what should she do?" Kathleen asked.

"I don't think she should worry about it," Alma said firmly. "If she's hesitating, it's because she feels there's something not quite right. Once she thinks it out, she'll know what to do."

"You aren't much help," Kathleen sighed, and then lifted her eyes and grinned at Alma. "I mean, this girl at school isn't going to get much good out of that gem of advice."

Alma grinned back at her. "But on the other hand, this girl at school has been expecting me to wave a magic wand and solve her problems for all these years. It's high time she started thinking things out for herself."

Kathy jumped up and hugged her. "Oh, Alma, you're so nice. I don't know how we'll get along without you."

"It isn't as if I'll be living on the other side of the moon," Alma pointed out. "I'll be right here in town."

"I know. But you'll have your own problems and your own family to take care of. The girl at school would feel pretty silly dumping all her troubles in your lap."

They smiled at one another—a warm smile that said everything that needed to be said. Why, she wouldn't really be losing Alma. Alma would be close for as long as she needed her—all she had to do was hold out her hand.

Alma glanced at the kitchen clock. "Tonight's the big night," she reminded Kathleen. "Better get your hair up, and then you can swish up the dishes while I work up a laundry list."

Kathleen stood in the wings as the members of the cast took their final curtain calls. The curtain had gone up and down, and up and down several times. Then, abruptly, the applause died away to a spatter, and it was over.

Kathleen hugged Margie and told her that she was wonderful, and that the audience had loved her. "You'll probably go on and be a big star," she told her friend. "And I'll be able to say I knew you when. . . ."

Marge was glowing. She hadn't ever looked so pretty, but Kathleen noticed that her eyes kept darting around as people came backstage to congratulate the players. She expects Bruce

173

to come back and congratulate her, Kathleen told herself, and felt again that twinge of guilt that had been bothering her.

She went to the dressing rooms to help some of the girls change out of their costumes and get ready for the cast party. Margie sat at the big dressing table, still the center of attention. She chattered and giggled, and when someone came to the door and passed in a florist box, she held both hands up before her face and pretended to hide. "Not another one," she mourned aloud. "I have *three* already." And she did—three neat little florist boxes marching along the top of the dressing table.

"This one is for Kathleen," said Mrs. David, and passed the box to Kathy, who took it reluctantly.

It was almost certain to be from her family. No one had ever sent her flowers before. She could read the card and tuck it into her blouse, but there was something dishonest about doing that, and besides, someone was almost sure to ask who the flowers were from. What could she say?

She took the card from the envelope while the other girls exclaimed over a perfectly huge white orchid.

"Who's it from, Kathy?" one of the girls demanded eagerly. "Did you ever see a more beautiful orchid in your life?"

Kathy turned the card over. *For Kathy*, it

said in bold, black print—but there was no signature, none at all. This was worse than ever. Everyone would think she'd sent it to herself!

"It isn't signed," she said helplessly. "I won't even know who to thank."

Mrs. David smiled and patted her shoulder. "Never mind, dear, whoever sent it will let you know. Maybe he was too shy to sign his name."

Kathleen smiled, a secret smile. "No, I don't think he was too shy. I think . . . I think maybe this is a belated valentine."

She took the lovely corsage and held it against her shoulder. Marge was watching her with suspicion in her blue eyes. "Don't you really have any idea who it could be from?"

"A very flimsy idea," Kathleen admitted. "I could be wrong."

They went to the cast party, which was held in the girls' gym. When Kathy came back from the locker room, after hanging up her coat, the first person she saw was Swede. His face lighted up when she smiled at him, and then darkened again when Bruce sauntered up.

"You look good enough to eat without cream or sugar," Bruce greeted her. "Doesn't she, Swede?"

Swede nodded miserably. "Yeah, she sure does."

The dancing started almost at once, and Marge was the belle of the ball, as was to be expected. She was very gay and her laughter bubbled like a fountain, but Kathleen, who knew her so well, saw the bleakness in her friend's eyes and recognized the note of near-hysteria in her voice.

Bruce was practically the only boy at the party who didn't ask Marge to dance. But he danced constantly with Kathleen, and when Kathy went to the locker room to freshen her lipstick, Marge followed her. She regarded her friend bitterly as she pretended to rearrange her hairdo.

"You and Bruce seem to be quite a twosome," she said, when it became obvious that Kathleen wasn't going to bring up the matter. "I suppose you know he's only giving you a big rush to spite me."

"He didn't mention it," Kathleen said politely. "Why would he want to spite you, Margie?"

"I don't know," Margie snapped. She turned her head away so that Kathleen couldn't see her face. But her hands were unsteady as she picked up her comb and lipstick and thrust them back into her purse. She left the room without another word.

Kathleen went back to the dance floor, feeling oddly shaken. At once Bruce was beside her, whirling her out onto the floor, and then through the opened doors onto the tennis courts that were strung with Japanese lanterns to give a party effect.

There were several other couples walking around hand in hand, but Bruce took Kathleen's arm and piloted her to a quiet corner. "How soon can we duck this affair?" he asked.

She looked up at him gravely. "Bruce, I . . . I don't think I should go tonight. But if you'd like to come over tomorrow—"

He looked at her blankly. "Tomorrow? Why?"

"I thought you might like to come to dinner. It's Sunday."

"I know it's Sunday," he said impatiently. "I'm going out to the lake with some of the guys. Chris has a new boat and some water skis."

"Oh," said Kathleen, in a very small voice. "Well, maybe some other time then."

He looked at her dubiously. "Look, are you playing games with me?"

She shook her head. "Oh no. I wouldn't do that."

He grinned then, his all-conquering grin. "Why not—Valentine?"

Kathleen could tell that she was blushing. "You knew it all the time, didn't you?"

He laughed. "How could I help it? Every time I turned around, there you were, looking at me with all those eyes. The fellows used to kid me about it."

"I'm sorry," she said.

"Don't be sorry. I kind of enjoyed it." His

dark eyes were laughing at her, and his shoulders cut off her escape.

"I think we'd better go back inside," Kathy whispered. "They seem to be making some announcements."

"Well, good for them." He didn't even glance around to see if they were being observed. He took her roughly by the shoulders and pulled her forward and kissed her—a long, deliberate kiss.

She stood very still with her eyes closed, waiting for the enchantment to begin, but nothing happened. A boy, a very special boy, had given her her first grown-up kiss, and she didn't feel anything except embarrassment. What if one of the chaperons walked out and saw them? She pulled away from him and turned her head aside.

Bruce's hands dropped from her shoulders immediately. "Now what's the matter?" he demanded. "Didn't you want me to kiss you?"

She almost could have smiled at the resentment in his voice. He really couldn't imagine a girl not wanting him to kiss her. She remembered a line from a television show, and it came out with exactly the right note of polite boredom. "I just don't like being mauled," she said.

Bruce looked so furious that she wanted to giggle. He reached into his jacket pocket and pulled out a package of cigarettes, and when

178

someone came charging out onto the court, Bruce looked at Kathy over the flare of the match. "I think your blunderfoot boy friend is coming to rescue you from a fate worse than death," he observed flippantly.

"He isn't—" Kathy started to say that Swede wasn't her boy friend, but instead she said, "—he isn't a blunderfoot."

Swede came over and stood beside them, looking huge and awkward and troubled. "Is everything O.K.?" he asked.

"Everything's just dandy." Bruce clapped him on the shoulder lightly. "Be a good Joe and take over for me, will you? I've got to see a girl about a date."

He walked away without even a backward glance at Kathleen. Swede shifted from one foot to the other, looking as if he would have been more comfortable in a dentist's chair.

"I'm sorry," he said at last. "I always seem to be barging in where I'm not wanted."

Kathleen gave him a wobbly smile. "It's the silliest thing," she gulped, "but when you came charging up like that I expected you to ask me if . . . if the gentleman was annoying me. You know, like in the old-time movies."

"Well, *was* he annoying you?" It was somehow endearing that Swede had missed the point altogether. "Because if he was, I'll take him apart bone by bone."

"It won't be necessary," Kathleen assured

him. "You can do something for me, though. You can drive me home. All of a sudden my feet hurt, and I'm beginning to remember how long it's been since I got up this morning."

"Sure, I'll be glad to drive you home. You get your coat and stuff and I'll go out and get the station wagon warmed up."

She went back inside to collect her belongings and say good night to the hostesses. Bruce was dancing with another girl, a senior who was new in town. He was smiling down at her and whispering against her hair.

Kathy looked at him and sighed. If he weren't so good-looking, it wouldn't be so hard. All these years she had been telling herself that Bruce was someone very special and important in her life. There would be a large vacancy in her daydreams for a while—and maybe she would never again meet anyone like him. He looked up and saw her watching him and his eyebrows lifted.

She remembered that he had said, "Every time I turned around, there you were, looking at me with all those eyes."

Kathleen turned quickly and went into the locker room to get her coat, but once she had it in her hands she wanted nothing so much as to put her face down against the soft material and let the threatening tears come. She didn't, though; instead she lifted her chin and moved to the small mirror on the wall. But her hands were unsteady as she smoothed on fresh lipstick and ran a comb through her hair.

You can't cry here, she told herself fiercely. If you can just manage to smile while you walk out to the car, and wait until after Swede has gone home and you've said good night to Dad and Mother and Alma, if you can just get through the next fifteen or twenty minutes. . . . She lifted the corners of her mouth into a smile and went out to meet Swede.

They drove to her house in almost complete silence, but she was aware that Swede kept shooting worried little glances in her direction.

He ran around the car to let her out, and then walked up to the porch with her. "Thanks for bringing me home," Kathy said carefully. "I'd ask you to come in except . . . except that it's so late."

Swede shifted from one large foot to the other. "That's all right. I should be getting on home anyway." He hesitated, and then rushed on. "I was wondering if it would be all right if I dropped by to see you tomorrow sometime."

She looked at him seriously. "Of course it would be all right." Then she heard herself add, "Or better still, why don't you come for dinner? We usually eat around four on Sunday. You can call after church and let me know."

"Are you sure it will be all right with your family?"

"Of course I'm sure," Kathy said, and knew as she uttered the words that they were true. "Anyway, I'm on kitchen detail tomorrow, so maybe you aren't getting such a bargain."

His blue eyes were warm and happy. "That's swell then. I'll call you after church." He turned and started down the steps, but her voice halted him.

"Swede?"

"Hm?"

"The flower—the orchid was from you, wasn't it?"

She had to ask. Maybe she already knew the answer, but she had to ask. She didn't know whether she was glad or sorry when he lifted his shoulders in a self-conscious shrug.

"It was sweet of you," Kathy said, over the lump in her throat. "Only you're supposed to sign the card."

He scowled faintly. "I did. I wrote *To Kathy* on it."

She wanted to laugh, but a wobbly smile was all she could manage. "But Swede, you're supposed to sign your name. So the girl will know who the flowers are from."

He looked at her with his heart in his eyes. "I thought you'd know it was from me," he said simply. "Anyway, next time I'll remember to sign my name."

She went into the house and closed the door gently behind her, as though any noise might shatter her self-control. Wimpy, who was still watching television, looked up at Kathleen, but she just nodded at him and tiptoed out into the kitchen, where she unpinned her corsage and put it carefully in the refrigerator.

Alma followed her almost at once. "Your mother and father went over to the Chessmans' for a while. Some of the parents are celebrating the play's being over."

Kathleen nodded. "That's nice," she said listlessly.

Alma gave her a sharp glance that saw past all the surface evasions, and then transferred her attention to the corsage. "It's a beautiful orchid, Kathy. I don't think I ever saw a prettier one."

"I'll wear it to church tomorrow," Kathleen said. She closed the refrigerator and turned to look at Alma. "I'm pretty tired. I guess I'll go right up to bed."

Alma's eyes softened. "Of course, honey. Good night."

Kathleen undressed in the darkness and climbed into bed, turning her face into the cool comfort of her pillow. She felt a hundred years old, and her throat ached, but the tears that had been pushing against her eyelids refused to come. She kept remembering the evening in flashes—the turmoil in the dressing room after the performance, and the moment when she had held the corsage box in her hands and tried so hard to believe that the flower was from Bruce. She remembered Margie's accusing eyes and Swede's wooden smile as she had danced again and again with Bruce; she recalled the utter humiliation of the moment when she had invited Bruce to Sunday dinner and he had shrugged it off and told her he was going up to the lake with some of the fellows. She detoured around thinking about the kiss that should have been so special and was instead a disillusionment.

She had been certain that she wouldn't be able to sleep a wink, so she was startled when she wakened much later in the darkness, aware that someone was moving about quietly, hanging up the dress she had tossed over a chair, putting away the high-heeled shoes she had kicked aside.

At first she thought it was Alma, but the figure was too slight, and a faint perfume seemed to reach out of the past and nudge at Kathleen's memory. "Mother?" she whispered, and at once her mother crossed to the bed and smiled down at her in the faint light from the hallway.

"I'm sorry I wakened you. I was going to ask about the party, but you were so sound asleep I hadn't the heart to disturb you."

Kathleen struggled up on one elbow. "It . . . it was a nice party," she said. "I got my very first orchid."

"I know. I saw it in the refrigerator."

"And I got my very first kiss," Kathleen thought wryly. "I'll bet you didn't see *that* in the refrigerator."

Her mother was still standing there watching her. She put out her hand, touched Kathy's cheek, and spoke softly. "What's wrong, dear?"

Kathleen sat up and hugged her knees to her chest, and the tears that had been dammed up all evening started slipping down her cheeks. "I don't know what's the matter with me," she gulped. "I just don't know, but I'm so miserable I could *die*. I do everything wrong, Mother. I don't think I'm going to like being grown-up. . . ."

Her mother's hand was very gentle, moving across her head. "Being grown-up takes getting used to, just like everything else. Remember when you started to kindergarten, Kathy? You'd looked forward to it for such a long time, and then when we finally had you enrolled you hated it and cried to stay home." She waited a moment, and then went on. "But after a little while you loved going to school."

Kathy brushed away a tear with the back of her hand and spoke in a strangled voice. "I don't know what makes me such an idiot."

"Do you want to talk about it?" her mother asked. "Sometimes it helps to clear the air."

Kathy started to say no, that she didn't want to talk about it or even think about it, but instead she heard herself blurting out the whole story, beginning with the valentine she had sent Bruce in the sixth grade. Her mother didn't interrupt or comment, she just listened. When Kathleen got to the part about Bruce kissing her, she didn't look surprised or the least bit shocked.

"So then—so then he had the nerve to ask me what was the matter, didn't I *want* him to kiss me, as if no girl could be that stupid."

Kathy looked up and saw that her mother was smiling very faintly. "What did you say to that?" she prompted.

"I said . . . I told him that I didn't want him to kiss me . . . but I guess I did."

Her mother nodded, as if this made perfectly good sense. "It sounds to me as if you handled the situation very well, honey." She added quietly, "He'll come back, you know."

Kathleen thrust down the little flicker of hope the words gave her. She didn't want Bruce to come back—not really. The dream-prince Bruce, yes—but not the tall young man who had looked at her with such arrogance in his dark eyes, who had said, "Look, are you playing games with me?"

She didn't want him to come back. Did she?

Her mother seemed to be reading her mind with uncanny accuracy. "And when he does come back," she concluded mildly, "you'll know what to do about it."

Kathleen slid down onto the pillow again, and

her mother tucked the blanket up around her shoulder before she leaned over and dropped a swift kiss on her daughter's cheek. The perfume was as faint as a remembered lullaby. "Good night, Kathy."

"Good night, Mother." Kathleen surprised herself by yawning, and then spoke in a dreamy voice that already trembled on the edge of sleep. "You still wear that same perfume, don't you? The kind you wore when you used to tuck me in. It's funny, isn't it, how your nose can remember a scent for years and years?"

"It's funny," her mother said, "how much the heart can remember."

She heard her mother go into Wimpy's room, and then, a little later, she heard her going down the stairs.

Kathy crossed her arms under her head and stared into the darkness, willing herself to stay awake because there was so much she wanted to think about now, while everything was clear.

Alma. She'd try to be really happy for Alma when she married and left them. She'd make a determined effort to be friends with the Graham children.

And she'd stop being cross with Wimpy, who was a boy and couldn't help being such a problem.

She'd insist that her mother play tennis and go shopping with her. There was something else, too . . . oh yes. Her mother played the piano. It would be nice having someone play the piano again. Maybe Father would turn the old upright in on one of the new spinets.

And then, just before she fell asleep, she remembered that Swede had said *next time* he'd remember to sign his name. She smiled and then sighed, a slow, shuddering sigh that seemed to come from her toes. She turned her face against her pillow, and finally slept.